# the country club

# ELIZABETH BROMKE

This book is a work of fiction. Names, characters, places, and events are products of the author's imagination. Any resemblance to locations, events, or people (living or dead) is purely coincidental.

Copyright © 2020 Elizabeth Bromke

All rights reserved.

Cover design by Red Leaf Book Design

The reproduction or distribution of this book without permission is a theft. If you would like to share this book or any part thereof (reviews excepted), please contact us through our website:

elizabethbromke.com

THE COUNTRY CLUB

Publishing in the Pines

White Mountains, Arizona

## CHAPTER 1—MERYL

Meryl Preston snapped a fresh flame to life along the striker of a new matchbox. She preferred matches to lighters. The wispy, heady smoke trailing into the air added to her relaxation.

Cupping a hand around her cinnamon-apple candle, Meryl drew the little fire to the wick before dousing the half-charred stick in the bathwater and flicking it expertly to the nearby wastebasket.

Then, she perched the fragrant candle on the edge of her garden tub. Finally, with everything just *so*, Meryl shrugged off her terry cloth robe and hung it on its hook before clawing her long, dishwater-blonde hair into a clip. At last, she eased down into the Epsom salt bubble bath.

A pleasant sigh escaped the forty-year-old's lips as the warm water overtook her, seeping up her neck into her hairline.

Meryl loved a good bubble bath. It had the power to wash away not just the daily grime but also the daily stress. Teaching seventh-grade math was no easy task, and it was Meryl's firm belief that if she was expected to do her job well, then she'd better set herself up for success. Thus, the nightly bath-time ritual.

After twenty minutes of soaking, she drained the tub, rubbed thick cream into her face, massaged body oil onto her arms and legs, and slipped into a fresh pair of pajamas. With her outfit for the next day laid out and her students' final tests half graded, Meryl felt it more than appropriate to pop a TV dinner into the microwave, pluck her magazine from the coffee table, and snuggle into the recesses of her sofa as she tuned into yet another guilty pleasure: *Murder, She Wrote*.

At ten-fifteen that evening, her phone rang.

Meryl popped up from the sofa, suspicious about the late-night call.

"Hello?" she asked as she cradled the cordless black phone into the nook of her neck and hit the mute button on her TV remote.

"Meryl. It's Mom."

Meryl's heart skipped a beat. "Mom? Is everything okay?" She hated these sorts of calls. Late ones with hushed tones and short greetings.

"Yes. Everything is *great*," Gladys Preston emphasized the *great*, and Meryl realized it wasn't a hushed tone. It was her mother's excitable one, brimming with anticipation.

"Mom, it's past ten. What's up?"

Meryl was not particularly close with her parents. Or, rather, they were not particularly close with *Meryl*. At least, that's how things had grown among the family of three. As soon as Meryl had turned eighteen and taken the bus to college, the Prestons had checked her off their list and moved onto the next project. And there was always another project in the Prestons' lives. A charitable one, usually.

That would all be well and good if it hadn't strained their relationship with their daughter into oblivion.

Then again, things weren't *that* strained. Not if Gladys could pick up the phone at quarter past ten to give her daughter a modicum of good news.

"Meryl," her mother went on, "We're going on a *pilgrimage*."

"Mom," she replied, her eyebrows pricking together at the bridge of her nose, "a *pilgrimage*?"

"The Children of Fatima Foundation. Your dad and I just got the invitation. We're heading to the airport now. A redeye flight, if you can believe that. We're going to Rome. *Rome*, Meryl. But there's a problem, sweetheart."

The kicker. Meryl knew these moments all too well. "Okay..." she replied slowly.

"We're supposed to close on the Sussex apartments tomorrow at noon. Final walk-through. The keys. Everything, hon."

Not only were the Prestons voracious philanthropists, but they were also compulsive property investors, amassing rental properties the state over. It's how they funded their Christian exploits, naturally. Meryl was in on these investments well into her thirties. But once they turned the projects from simple flips to full-blown *rentals*, she checked out. She was *done*. Done driving two hours to the next town to handle a water leak. Done calling ten different electricians, begging down the rate for a new breaker. *Done*.

"No," Meryl answered. "I can't."

"But *Meryl*—"

"It's the end of the school year, Mom. I'd have to get a sub. Write plans. It's more work than it's worth. Sussex is over an hour from here." She squeezed her eyes shut, the pull of exhaustion tugging on her brain. "I'm sorry. I can't." Meryl moved the phone to her other ear and unmuted the television, settling back into the cushions, ready to pick up where she left off.

"Meryl, *please*. We… listen. We *need* this property. We *told* them tomorrow."

"Why do you *need* it, Mom? You have, what? Five now? Five complexes? Six including the one in Gull's Landing?"

"That's not a complex," Gladys replied. "And we're down to three complexes. Two are fully let, but we need more, Meryl."

"How can you manage more?" Meryl's eyes stung from the late hour. The long day. The annoying call.

"You really won't go?" her mother asked, sighing in defeat.

Meryl hesitated. She'd said yes for so long that saying no still didn't feel like an option. Even when she'd said it twice. Three times. By the fourth or fifth time—she got weak.

"One hour there, quick walkthrough, one hour back. You can start the school day, leave for a couple of hours, and make it back before dismissal, if you drive with a purpose."

Angela Lansbury came back on the screen. Meryl turned the volume up. "Sorry, Mom. I'm really sorry."

And then, she hung up the phone.

But that night, she didn't sleep. Not one wink. It was as though her body knew to expect the second call. The call she'd get hours later, before the sun rose. Before she had a chance to take back what she said. To say *yes*. Like she should have.

## CHAPTER 2—DELIA

Delia Astor took a seat at her usual table in the clubhouse, smoothing her rosy copper bob and sucking her lips into her mouth. She drew her pinky finger down her cupid's bow, ensuring her red lipstick hadn't smudged up towards her nose, then ordered a Petite Syrah. Handing the menu back to the waiter without so much as a glance, Delia thanked him and unfolded her napkin, tucking it around her slight thighs like a little blanket.

She was early. Always early. Her dear friend and neighbor, Nancy, wouldn't arrive for at least ten minutes, but that was all right. It gave Delia the chance to start her drink and admire the view from her window seat.

The clubhouse dining room of The Landing was situated on the ninth hole of its golf course. From her position there, Delia might catch a glimpse of her husband, Bryant, should he and the other members of his foursome arrive to putt before Delia and Nancy had wrapped up their brunch.

It was one of those fun things about marriage—having the chance to spy on her husband in his natural habitat. However, it seemed as though Delia's friends were past that stage in their own marriages. Or maybe they'd never enjoyed it to begin with. What with everyone *working* in a *career* or raising children, they always seemed to be in a bit of a whirlwind of their own making. Blustery whirlwinds that only ever deposited them momentarily at Delia's front stoop or in the seat opposite her. Blowing in and out of her life like falling red maple leaves in autumn, caught on this breeze or that.

Other people had a lot going on, that was for sure.

All Delia had was a husband and her presidency at the HOA. And cultivating the perfect, country club image that had so eluded her growing up as a boardwalk brat in Wildwood. It was no wonder Delia was content to tend to her life of peace and elegance. She'd fought hard for it, earning it just as those other women had earned their promotions or their motherhood or even their own husbands.

At least, though, Delia's husband was the greatest catch in all of Gull's Landing. Perhaps all of the Jersey Shore. A banking executive with a penchant for great cars and good clothes—Bryant Astor was the pinnacle of Delia's existence. Delia, the would-be homemaker. A homemaker, she'd become. Even if home never felt quite like home without children.

"Delia," Nancy squealed from halfway across the dining room as she stalked to their table in narrow green heels. "Am I late?"

"You're never late, Nancy." Delia pointed to Nancy's rosé. "It's not too early for you, is it? If so, I'll send it back—" Delia immediately looked for a waiter to snap over.

"No, no!" Nancy protested. "Katherine is away for an overnight babysitting charge from now until tomorrow evening. All I have is some unpacking to do, and *that* can wait."

Nancy was recently divorced and simply *thriving*. She and her teen daughter had moved into The Landing at the behest of another of her friends, Betsy Borden, a woman Delia admired for her strength of deposition.

Delia and Nancy had met at a gala the previous year—a fundraiser for endangered animals of the Atlantic seaboard. Bryant had donated. Nancy had organized. She and Delia had hit it off *immediately* over their shared drive and hobbies, particularly their common interest in what Nancy called *a life of luxury*. Coming from a similar background also contributed to their fast friendship. And it was that very background—rough and tumble and marred by pain—that resulted in Nancy's refusal to stay in her marriage, despite the potential financial consequences of a divorce. With a bully for a father, she'd demanded better for herself, rising above what she was trained to accept and demanding *more*. It's also how she'd managed to purchase a home in The Landing. That *drive*.

Even though Nancy was Delia's best friend, Delia often suspected that *she* was not *Nancy's* best friend. A woman like Nancy didn't seem to have a best friend. Rather, she had lots of *girlfriends*. And then, naturally, there was her daughter. In Nancy's world, Katherine came first. *Always*, she'd emphasized.

Sometimes, Delia wondered if an appointment as the HOA president and a sexy, successful husband was *enough*. If what she had was *enough*.

Nancy spoke, snapping Delia from her reverie. "I've only got half an hour, though. I'm meeting with Norman Grimwood to interview him for a piece in the *Gazette*." She threw her hands up and laughed. "I'm *too* busy, Delia! I *really* am."

Delia lifted an eyebrow but forced a compassionate smile. "You poor thing. All you do is work. I can't imagine." She could, though. As her mother's only daughter, she'd done nothing *but* work all growing up. Together, they had cleaned homes from the time Delia was old enough to lift a toilet brush.

Delia lifted her Syrah to her lips, her French tips sparkling beside her wine glass. Maybe, just maybe, the good life *was* enough.

Nancy took a long sip of her drink, too, then gazed at Delia. "*Dee*-lia," she said, over-enunciating the first syllable. "What are *you* up to today?"

"Oh, me?" Delia feigned casualness. "Well, I'll probably tidy up the house a bit. I have my book club this evening. I need to prepare a dish for that. I'm *hosting* this month."

"Oh, right. Right. You told me about that. What book did you read again?" Nancy was bored. A non-reader, she'd flitted in and out of the Boardwalk Book Club for years now.

Delia took another sip and glanced out the window, searching for Bryant. "*The Color Purple*."

"Oh yes. It was an instant classic, I heard," Nancy

mused as she narrowed her gaze out the window, too. "And *you're* hosting? The girls are going to *drool*, Deel," she added. "I doubt any one of them will ever want you to host again after they spend an evening in Chateau Astor."

Delia waved her off. "Oh, please."

Nancy glanced at Delia then dropped her chin. "You have *the home* in The Landing. It's your pride and joy!" Nancy cried then looked again out the window. "Isn't that Bryant's usual group on the green?"

Following Nancy's pointing index finger, Delia leveled her stare at a foursome below. All four men were familiar to Delia—either from the bank or The Landing.

"Where's Bryant?" Nancy asked before taking a final sip of her wine then raising her hand for the waiter. "I thought you said he was on the course today?"

Delia leaned closer to the window, searching the green for his familiar form. His polo shirt. His thick head of ashy blonde hair. Anything that would hint at her Bryant.

He wasn't there.

She looked up at her friend. "Um." Delia swallowed and tried for a smile.

Nancy pursed her lips. "Want me to come back to your place with you?"

Delia shook her head. "No, no. Of course not. I'm— he's probably in a different foursome. Or maybe he got called into work."

Crossing her arms over her chest, Nancy continued to eye her. "Come with me today. I could use a little help."

"Help?" Delia's voice cracked, and she cleared her throat. "No, truly. I need to prepare for tonight. Book club.

*The Color Purple.* Eggplant." She was murmuring her mental to-do list as she scanned the surrounding edges of the ninth hole, willing Bryant into her view.

"Suit yourself," Nancy trilled, accepting the billfold from the waiter and sliding her card into the leather. "My treat this time. I really have to go. This could be my breakout piece."

"Breakout piece?" Delia tried to refocus, pushing aside thoughts of Bryant and the fact that this was the *third* time he wasn't where he was supposed to be.

"Oh, yes. They found a body at this dilapidated house off of Mill River Road. Talk of the town. Apparently, it's not the *owner's* body, either."

Delia blinked and took the last swig of her drink, swallowing it and dabbing her lips with a linen napkin. "So, what's the story, exactly?" she wondered aloud, partially interested. Mostly anxious.

Nancy studied her. "Come with me, Deel. Please. It'll do you good to have a bit of a distraction."

But Delia shook her head, her gaze wandering again out the window. "I'm already distracted."

## CHAPTER 3—LUCY

Lucy Spaur stood at the newel post on her second-floor landing.

A creaking staircase descended at her feet. Heavy red carpeting ran down the center of the wooden steps, cutting in at a sharp ninety degrees with every tread. She gripped her cane in her right hand, her arm trembling at the elbow as she steadied the rubber foot on the first step. With her left hand, she clutched the banister, inching along as she shifted her weight down to meet the cane. She repeated this process for five more steps before she needed a rest.

The phone had long since stopped ringing, but that didn't deter Lucy. She knew *exactly* who was calling.

Marcia. Her daughter.

Marcia called every morning but never at the same hour. It was her little trick to *test* her mother.

Lucy pursed her lips and took a breath before making it down another five steps. And then another. And soon enough she'd made it to the first floor, her energy renewed.

Shuffling to the telephone table that stood along the inside of the stairwell, Lucy followed her cat, Fiona, who darted ahead of her.

For a cat, Fiona was somewhat thoughtful. Then again, the little orange thing had long ago learned that to weave in and out of Lucy's legs could only result in catastrophe. A missed afternoon meal, for starters. A delay in the litter box change.

Still, Lucy preferred to think that Fiona's feelings were as sympathetic for her pet human as they were self-preserving.

She spun the familiar digits into the dial and held the black receiver to her ear.

"Hello?" her daughter's rattling voice filled Lucy's ear.

"Yes, dear. It's Mom."

"*Mother*," Marcia gasped. "Why didn't you answer? I thought something happened. Are you okay?"

"I'm *fine*, Marcia. Just fine. You called when I was in the powder room. Marcia, *truly*. I'm fine."

"Did you hear?"

"Hear what?" Lucy eyed the wooden chair she'd recently moved to the telephone table. With Marcia's phone calls becoming so regular, it made sense to create a little chatting nook, as she liked to think of it. Lowering herself into the chair, she held back from letting out a heavy breath, blowing the air through her teeth as quietly as she could as her daughter prattled on.

"They found a poor old woman. *Dead*. Mother, they found her *dead*. In Gull's Landing!"

"Slow *down*, Marcia. What on *earth* are you talking about?"

"I read about it in the paper this morning. The paper *here*. In Ocean City, for goodness' sake!"

"What did you read?" Lucy was curious now, she had to give Marcia that. She tried to recall if she'd picked up the paper that morning before remembering that this was the first she'd been downstairs at all. Naturally, she had *not* read the paper. She hadn't even collected it from the stoop yet.

"A morning jogger was running along Mill River with his dog. His dog dashed off into this abandoned-looking house, you see. The man went after his dog and *inside* the house—the back door was left cracked open. Mom, *please* tell me you're locking your doors."

"I am," Lucy confirmed slowly, glancing at the front door to see the chain hanging in a straight line down the wall. She winced to herself and made a mental note to remember to lock up that night. Lucy was normally good at locking up. It was, after all, part of her routine. But the night before, she'd watched Dateline—which was *not* part of her routine. It threw everything off track and even gave her nightmares. One would think it would have had the opposite effect. That she'd have buttoned the house down well. But no, she'd somehow missed that important evening duty.

"Anyway, he smelled something awful in the house and found the dog sniffing around a *corpse*."

"Oh my," Lucy replied, clicking her tongue and shaking her head. "What a shame. Did the paper say who it was?"

"The jogger?" Marcia asked.

"No. Well, yes, as a matter of fact. Although I don't know many joggers..."

"His name was—oh, just a minute." Lucy could hear her daughter shuffling papers. "No, no it doesn't say the name of the jogger. Just that he was out for a run with his dog is all."

"And the person?"

"The who?" Marcia answered.

"The dead person, dear. Who died?"

"Oh," Marcia answered, and again came the sound of her thumbing through the paper. "Well, that's just it. They don't even say. Probably haven't notified next of kin."

"What a shame." Lucy clicked her tongue and patted her white hair. Her tongue was dry. Actually, her entire mouth was a bit dry. She needed a glass of juice.

"Well, I'll see what the *Gazette* has to say about it and give you a call back if I learn anything," Lucy said, heaving up from the chair.

"Mother, that's not why I called."

"Oh?"

"No, Mom. Well, *yes*, I mean I did want to tell you about this. It's exactly why I called. Mom," Marcia's voice broke, and Lucy squeezed her eyes shut, lifting a hand to her forehead. *Here we go*, she thought. Marcia shuddered on the other end of the line before sniffling and finishing her thought. "Mom, this could have been *you*."

Lucy lifted her eyebrow at Fiona, who purred discontentedly.

Sure enough, Marcia was not going to drop it. And

now, here she was, scraping up some macabre tragedy as a way to threaten her own mother into doing what she wanted.

Still, Lucy knew how to play it. "How do you mean, Marcia?"

"If you died in your house, Mom, I may have to read about it in the *paper* for goodness' sake."

"Language, Marcia," Lucy trilled.

"Mom, seriously. You're all alone there. Someone could find you and I'd have to read about some old woman who was found dead in her house on First Street and I'd know it was you and that I was right."

"Right about what, Marcia?"

"That it's time, Mom. It's time for you to go to Golden Oaks."

## CHAPTER 4—MERYL

The funeral came and went swiftly.

Meryl blinked, and it was over. And she was *really* alone. Not the kind of alone that she'd grown accustomed to. The TV dinners and self-indulgent evenings. The kind of alone that left her chest hollow and her days empty. Even busy days had turned robotic. She now lived in a shell of her former existence.

And it all materialized in a matter of days. Days! Who knew life could change on a dime like that. Like a switch flipped, and everything Meryl figured to be normal... *poof*. A blown-out match. A spent flame.

Working through the administrative tasks of her parents' deaths proved easier than Meryl predicted. Not because the Prestons had been duly prepared for their own deaths, however. But because, well, they *hadn't*.

With so little to coordinate, the remnants of the Prestons' business ventures and personal effects became little more than currency. There would be little for Meryl to tend to now. No more emergency water leaks. No more final walk-throughs, either.

It turned out that her mother's final plea was sincere enough. Though Meryl doubted they were truly destitute, it became clear that her parents had needed a new rental property to help cover the bills of the other ones. How they could have secured financing for a new investment was a matter of knowing the right people in the right places. A *blind* banker here. A *distracted* lender there. And a relative for a realtor.

Aunt Viola.

She called her niece the Monday following the funeral, somehow getting patched through to Meryl's classroom from the front desk. Perhaps the secretary figured things were still touch-and-go. Perhaps she took great pity on Meryl's circumstances. Perhaps she figured Meryl *needed* to talk to her relatives in the wake of losing her parents so tragically—a freak car crash at the hands of a slovenly drunk driver.

Perhaps the secretary didn't realize that Meryl was running as far away from the pain and guilt and confusion as she could *get* and she had *no* interest in dealing with her father's sister.

"Meryl," Viola said into the phone, her voice devoid of emotion.

"Yes?"

"Has the lawyer been in touch?"

"Which lawyer would that be?" Meryl sat at her desk between class periods. She had to be there, of course. It was the last Monday of the school year. Final exams. Final marks. Final *everything*. Anyway, it was her escape.

Her refuge. The place she ran to when she needed to get away. Couldn't Viola have surmised as much when she tracked Meryl down to her place of employment? Apparently not. Or, just as likely, the matters of the Prestons' deaths and the mess they'd left behind were too great to consider their orphan daughter's heartache. To consider that Meryl required distance. Not proximity to it all.

"The estate man. He's been trying to reach out. Wrong number, perhaps. Listen, Meryl. To cover the debt, you'll have to let go of the Newark apartments and the Ocean City townhome. There's a chance you could salvage the property up north, if you have a mind to—"

"I don't." Meryl's tone was ice. "I don't have a mind to save any of it."

A brief pause pooled across the phone line. Meryl glanced at the doorway, where little faces crowded in, staring curiously at her.

"And now I have to go, Aunt Viola. Class is about to begin and—"

"Meryl," Viola replied, "There's just one more thing."

Meryl stood, ready to whisk her second-period students into the room and sweep them away in a lesson about factorials. "Go on," she directed her aunt.

"It's the house in Gull's Landing."

An exasperated sigh slipped through her lips and Meryl gave up on getting all the way off the line. She waved a hand to the two girls whose faces implored her to give them the green light to come in.

The class was loud. Too loud for so early in the morning, but that was seventh grade. They hadn't realized that morning hours were sleepy ones. Too excited. Too nervous. Too joyous to be among their peers and enemies in one melting pot of an educational institution.

"What house?" Meryl asked Viola, raising her voice and plugging one ear with her finger.

"There's a house in Gull's Landing."

"Gull's Landing?" Meryl twisted the town name over her tongue. "Gull's *Landing*?"

"Tiny little town on the boardwalk. Wedged in there between Wildwood and Ocean City," Viola went on.

"Yes, I know about Gull's Landing," Meryl confirmed, snapping her fingers at the class and pointing them into their seats. "My mother's hometown," she added.

"Right, yes. Well, they had a place there, and it's got no claims against it. No mortgage. Free and clear. And if you play it right, Meryl, you can save it."

"Save it?" *From what*, she wanted to add, but the conversation had to end. She had a number line to finish on the chalkboard and fidgeting adolescents to rein in. "Okay, listen Viola. I'll give you a call after school today. We'll make a plan then."

"It's more urgent than that," Viola answered, her tone sharp now.

Meryl curled her body away from the increasingly noisy group of children, tucking her chin low. "What do you mean 'urgent'?"

"There's been a—well, someone *died* in the house. They just found the body last week, I guess, and by the time they called your parents to follow up, it was too late, I suppose."

"How did they get in touch with you?" Meryl asked.

The surrounding chatter of students grew muted as the blood pounded in her ears.

"They didn't. They left a message on the answering machine, and I listened to it this morning when I was going through your parents' effects." Viola's voice came across as judgy and cool. It should be Meryl going through her parents' things. And she *would* be, too, that weekend. After taking a breather. Viola, for her part, was too nosey. Too curious. Too impatient.

And now, she was taking up too much of Meryl's time. "Whoever it is, I'm sure the local officials have it under control."

"Meryl," Viola hissed. "They need to interview the owners of the house."

"Well, they're dead," Meryl huffed, holding back a well full of tears deep in her chest.

"Your parents are, yes. But *you* own the house now. It's *you* they want to talk to."

"Well, I'm selling the house," Meryl replied, on the verge of hanging up on her aunt.

"Not yet, you're not. You can't sell that place until you've given the police your statement. The lawyers say so."

"A dead body isn't a lien," Meryl pointed out, her voice rising just enough that the back row of students whipped their heads round to eavesdrop. Meryl snapped her fingers at them and pointed to the board. "Turn around and start your bell work," she directed, casual as ever.

Viola snorted. "That may be, but the fact of the

matter is that you have to deal with it. At this rate, if someone else dies, you could be liable."

Meryl squeezed her eyes shut. "Who *died*?" she demanded again.

But Viola had beaten her to the punch. The line was dead. And Meryl had two choices: ignore the problem. Then, pluck away the possessions of her parents which she *did* want to keep. Or go to Gull's Landing. Talk to the police. Clean up the house and list it right away. At the very least, she could make a little money and move on with her life.

## CHAPTER 5—DELIA

"Bryant?" Delia called as she dropped her keys into the bowl on the glass table in the foyer. "I thought you were golfing?"

Her voice carried on an echo through their oversized house, bouncing along midrange artwork and department-store furniture. Just as soon as Bryant earned another raise, they'd be upgrading.

In the meantime, however, Delia made do. She'd arranged what they did own in a way that screamed *high end*. Luxury. Taste. Elegance. Glamor.

Money.

She knew how to play the country club game, and it showed.

It was in her casual gratitude when someone complimented her second-hand Prada clutch. *Vintage*, she'd remark with a smirkish grin.

It was in her look—the clean lines of her outfits, free of designer labels but still so sleek.

It was in her upkeep—dabbing rosewater at her pulse

points. Scrubbing behind her ears until the thin skin there was raw and red. Cleaning the nooks and crannies of her body, tending to it like a fire engine. Washing her hair every other day and blowing it out like a professional. Appearing at the salon every six weeks, as scheduled. Keeping her nail appointments without exception. All the things she didn't do as a girl. All the things she'd never dreamed of doing. She clung to these routines with her might, as though her very livelihood depended on French tips and red lips.

It was in her coy dismissal of the oohs and ahhs when a guest dropped by for a visit. *Oh, please. It's just a house!*

But the Astor home was not just a house. It was the one thing that truly did divide Bryant and Delia from their peers. As a banking person, he had some money, yes. Not enough, however, to buy the biggest house in The Landing, to be sure.

No, no.

They had managed to acquire 639 Albatross Avenue in a *foreclosure*. Not everyone in town knew this little secret. They didn't know that it was, effectively, a budget property, purchased by Bryant alone—the prenuptial arrangement accounted for the fact that he'd be the one to make the purchases and with him those same purchases would remain. This hadn't mattered to Delia because she couldn't fathom a life without Bryant, just as he'd sworn he couldn't fathom a life without her.

The prenup was to protect *Delia*, he'd insisted. Just in case. She'd accepted that, eager to marry him. To be with him. But her acceptance didn't mean she didn't often think about it. Though, she never ever *once* spoke of it.

Most of Delia's friends had no idea about that pesky little prenup, either.

But they did know that Delia had fussed and fiddled until she'd updated the 1940s Victorian abode into a sparkling new spectacle—both reminiscent of its original glory and promising of a fashionable future. They knew she was the brains behind the operation. The artist, too.

"Bryant?" she sang out again, winding down the hall and into the kitchen, where she fully expected to find him, on a last-minute work call. Some disaster at the office or one of the branches. Something that had torn him away from his tee time.

He wasn't there.

Delia swiveled on her heel, clacking back down the parquet-floored hall and to the staircase. She gripped the banister with trepidation, unsure if she *really* wanted to go upstairs. *Really* wanted to see if her husband was there. In their bedroom.

Or perhaps a guest room.

He had to be there *somewhere*. His car was sitting in the garage. The hood cool to the touch.

"Bryant?" Delia trilled up the stairs as she slowly climbed, pulling herself up each step with the very tips of her fingers, her heart racing.

Once she arrived on the landing, she stalled, her shoes settling quietly on the oriental rug that ran the length of the second-floor corridor.

Holding her breath, she listened very, very carefully.

Nothing.

Two steps toward the master bedroom, she could have sworn she heard a bed creak.

Her head twisted toward the guest bedroom to her left, and she took one silent step toward it.

Another beat and Delia's hand was on the door and she was pushing it open wide. Inside, the guest bed. Made. Untouched.

Delia released her breath and clutched her chest, then strode to the window to the right of the bed. She cranked it open, gasping for fresh air.

When her breathing and pulse had returned to normal, her eyes flitted down into the backyard, a perfectly square patch of green glowing up in between planters filled with flowers. Between the grass and the house, she saw him. Bryant.

Alone.

In his hand, he held what appeared to be pages. Pure, white pages. From Delia's vantage point at the window, they could have held anything. Figures for work. A fax. *Anything*. The sinking feeling in the pit of her stomach, however, told her they weren't some work figures. They weren't some fax.

When she made her way back downstairs, as slowly as she'd made her way *up*stairs, he'd beat her into the kitchen. And it was there that she found out exactly *what* those pages were. By then, naturally, Bryant was long gone.

And Delia was about to be long gone, too.

After all, the house was Bryant's. The house and everything in it. Everything, now, except for Delia.

## CHAPTER 6—LUCY

Lucy shook the paper out at her kitchen table and adjusted her eyeglasses. Fiona purred at her feet, languidly dragging lazy eights around the old woman's ankles.

The story Marcia had referenced blared across the front page of the *Gazette*.

"Body Found in Mill River House."

The byline belonged to Nancy Shytle. Lucy Spaur didn't much care for Nancy Shytle on account of the fact that it was Nancy Shytle who had coordinated the opening of Golden Oaks Senior Living.

Lucy clicked her tongue, sad for the headline and irritated for the byline, and read on.

*During a morning jog, Gull's Landing local Jane Gentry discovered the body of an unidentified female in a home along Mill River Road.*

Squinting up from the paper, Lucy ran the name over her tongue and up to her brain. *Jane Gentry*. A woman jogger. How brave. But Lucy didn't know her. And what about the dog? Wasn't there a dog?

She returned to the article.

*Though many citizens consider the house in question to have been long abandoned, county records reveal that it belongs to a former resident of Gull's Landing, Gladys Preston.*

*Tragically, and perhaps coincidentally, Preston and her husband were killed in an apparently unrelated automobile collision just last week. Local law enforcement expects Preston's daughter, Meryl, to arrive in town to answer questions surrounding the events in the Mill River house.*

*If anyone has information regarding the case herein, he or she is directed to contact Gull's Landing Police Department at the non-emergency line.*

Lucy laid the paper back on the table and blew a slow whistle through her teeth. Once she'd processed the piece, she drew her teacup to her lips and took a cautious sip, so as not to burn her tongue. A tongue burn would be a bad start to the day. Then again, at least she was still alive to suffer it, should it happen. She really ought to count her blessings, as they said.

Marcia's threat crossed her mind and she eyed Fiona. "What do you think, Fiona?" Lucy asked the cat. "If I were locked away in Golden Oaks, would you stay on here? Keep this place in good condition for me?"

Fiona mewed irritably and pranced off.

She considered her daughter's opinion. Marcia did not believe Lucy could handle her own independence much longer. Any longer, as a matter of fact.

But Lucy wasn't senile. She wasn't lame, or dumb, or without basic human functions. It was much, *much* too soon for her to be stowed away in an old folks' home. No matter how cutesy the name of the place.

*Golden Oaks.* Harumph! Golden Oaks Lucy's behind!

An idea materialized in her still-intact brain, and Lucy pulled the newspaper back toward herself. She drew her thumb down her tongue, wetting the skin to make it sticky, then turned the pages of the periodical until she came upon the Classifieds section.

Pressing a finger down the rental housing column, Lucy read each submission, stopping at those which held a bit of promise. Perhaps a studio apartment near the hospital in Ocean City. Or a handicap-accessible one-bedroom.

Even so, she was left with the same problem: sure, Marcia probably worried about the front stoop and the staircase to the second floor. Mainly, however, her concern was that Lucy lived all alone.

There was another option. Something awkward and perhaps indecent in the modern age. It'd be highly rude of Lucy to even *hint* at that other option. But if Lucy was gung-ho about steering clear of Golden Oaks, then she may not have another choice.

No.

No, no, no.

Lucy would *never*. She would *never* be a burden. Not to Marcia. Not to anyone!

Apparently, though. She already was. No, not a physical burden. An emotional one. Marcia fretted over her mother. Much like Lucy had fretted over Marcia for so many years.

Maybe Lucy didn't have a choice. Maybe her only real

option was to ease her daughter's worries and give up the one thing she thought she still had, even in her old age: freedom.

## CHAPTER 7—MERYL

Meryl arrived in Gull's Landing Saturday afternoon. Viola promised to meet her at the funeral home, where they'd be asked to identify the remains of the person found in the house on Mill River Road. Gladys Preston's house, to be specific.

When Meryl asked why the body hadn't made a stopover at the county morgue, they'd replied that the county morgue was too far of a drive. They figured they'd handle things at Second Street Mortuary.

This was odd to Meryl. The handling of a suspiciously dead body at a funeral home. Yet, she had no idea how funeral matters really worked. So, she accepted it, parking behind the Second Street Mortuary sign and wondering how she'd arrived at a phase of life where parking at a funeral home was quickly turning commonplace.

A Jeep pulled up next to her.

Inside, a woman with wild tangles of silvery hair

waved through the open space where a car window would go. Viola's bejeweled fingers flashed red at the tips.

"Here we go." Viola didn't have to say much more. The two women had been together just the weekend prior, in similar, though much sadder, circumstances.

"Here we go," Meryl murmured in echo.

They walked together to the front door and Meryl opened it for her aunt, the heavy wood creaking. When she closed it behind them, it didn't latch immediately. Meryl had to finagle it shut.

No one was in the lobby to greet them, initially. Soon, however, a pale-faced man with thick spectacles poked his head out from an interior door. He smiled in a practiced, soft way. Gentle. His stride to them matched the smile: slow and unassuming. "Viola and Meryl," he said, not quite a question. Not quite a statement.

Meryl glanced at her aunt, who nodded. Meryl nodded, too.

"Norman Grimwood." The man took Viola's hand in both of his, holding it there briefly before doing the same with Meryl. His smile fell away. "I'm terribly sorry to hear of your loss." He said this to Meryl, primarily, and she appreciated that. She appreciated that he realized it was a touch more difficult for a child to lose a parent than for a sister to lose a brother.

But he wasn't so dense as to ignore Viola completely. "I'm so terribly sorry," he repeated for her benefit, too.

"Thank you," the women replied in unison.

"So," Norman clasped his hands together, "Chief Grigsby is in the back with Emily, my embalmer." He turned and released his hands, lifting one toward the back of the building. "Shall I show you the way?"

They followed, and all the potential for awkwardness and bizarreness somehow driveled away.

Meryl cleared her throat, hoping to get a head-start on proceedings so that she could get back home. Summer break stretched ahead of her, and there was no reason she ought to stick around Gull's Landing. Not with Viola there to handle the house. "Mr. Grimtree," she said.

"Grimwood," he politely corrected. "But please, call me Norm."

"I'm sorry." Meryl flushed. She was normally very good with names. An occupational hazard. Filtering through 150 students a day, she had no other choice. Her tag itched at the back center of her collar. Heat swept into a line of sweat along her spine. "Norm," she went on. "I'm sure I won't know this man."

"Woman," he corrected with a grimace.

"Woman?" Viola chirped. "It was a woman who died there?"

"Yes. And to your point, Miss Preston—" Norman indicated Meryl "—I didn't think you would know her."

Unsure what to say, Meryl didn't reply to him. Instead, they wove into an open doorway, through a silent, wood-paneled office, and entered a second, interior door.

Beyond that was their destination. A small, white-walled room. In one corner, a thick porcelain sink protruded from the wall, hanging low, with tentacles for faucets. A cabinet with a second, normal sink stood in the other corner.

Of course, the sinks were hardly a distraction from the haunting form of a body on a slab beneath a white sheet. Like a ghost laid to rest. Beyond the table with the tented white fabric, two people stood waiting. A youngish girl—perhaps in her twenties—and a middle-aged man. The chief.

Norman made introductions, but Meryl and Viola declined to shake hands with the others, as they'd be forced to reach across the sad centerpiece of the room. That would be awkward and perhaps even disrespectful. Macabre at the very least.

"Meryl, Viola," Chief Grigsby said, his use of their first names a result of their shared last name, perhaps. Or maybe it was a small-town effect. Immediate intimacy. "Thank you both for coming, particularly on the heels of your own personal tragedy." He ran his hand along his jaw, awkward at the transition into business.

"We're fairly certain we know who this woman is, but seeing as she'd been in the house for so long, it appeared, we want to ensure she might not be kin to you folks."

Meryl's eyebrows crimped together. If they figured they knew who she was, then what did they need Meryl for? Or Viola?

Chief Grigsby nodded to the girl—introduced as Miss Addams—and she pinched the corners of the sheet, tugging it down to the woman's chin.

Viola gasped theatrically, fanning her face with her hand.

Meryl leaned in closer.

"Nope," she said after inspecting the gray, lined face. Heavy hollows bled from beneath the open eyes. Open and creamy. The woman's skin sagged into her ears and down across where her jawline ought to be. Though thinnish, her face appeared… soggy. "I don't know her."

"Viola?" Chief Grigsby pressed. "Is she familiar to you?"

Viola was peering out of one cracked eye, but Meryl knew this was for show. The woman had barged her way into her brother's and sister-in-law's embalming sessions to inspect and ensure they looked exactly as they should for the open casket, despite the fact that the mortician in Newark had cautioned against an open casket, mind you.

Shaking her head and looking away into the upper corner of the room, Viola answered, "No. Never seen her before in my life."

"Then, she's exactly who we figured she was." Chief Grigsby hitched his waistband higher onto his paunchy gut and gave a short nod to Norman.

Meryl couldn't help it. She was curious. "And who is that?" she asked.

The police chief tugged a packet of cigarettes from his breast pocket. "She's *nobody*."

## CHAPTER 8—MERYL

Initially, Meryl had planned to leave. Viola would stay behind. Walk through the house. Lock it up. They'd get in touch with a realtor and that would be that.

But something niggled at Meryl.

Viola could tell. "A drink?"

"It isn't five yet," Meryl pointed out. A diluted protest.

"It's five somewhere on this damned planet," her aunt replied. "I know a place. C'mon."

Meryl followed her in her own car, turning down tight avenues—left, then right, then right again—until they arrived in a cramped back parking lot of a corner diner with red and white umbrellas poking out of its patio like a cocktail.

"Maeve's," Viola said as they strolled the narrow sidewalk toward the front. "Best diner in town."

"And how do *you* know?" Meryl sassed her aunt.

"I asked the cop when we went out for a cigarette."

Meryl shook her head and chuckled. "Is that all you asked?"

The older woman shrugged. "I might have inquired about his naked ring finger. You know me." She winked at Meryl and they entered the eatery, marveling at the glass case and the delectables within.

Within half an hour, they were seated, served, and Meryl had asked Viola at which motel she planned to stay. "In case it turns out I'm not in driving shape," she added casually.

"Motel?" Viola asked. "I'm not staying in a motel."

"I thought you were staying? To walk through the house?" Meryl was confused. They *had* agreed Viola would be the one to stay.

"Of course I'm staying. I'm staying there. *In* the house." She shoved her hand into her bag and withdrew a jangling pair of old-timey bronze keys, their finish dulled by time and grime. "Grabbed them from your folks' utility closet. They have nine hooks and twice as many keys in there. Each with a little paper label, see?" She pinched a beige rectangle and thrust it toward Meryl.

*12 Mill River Road*.

Meryl's mouth fell open. "You're *joking*."

"No." Viola dropped the keys back into her purse, and they splashed among whatever else was in there. She shoved a forkful of salad into her mouth, the corners wet with white cream. Ranch. "They were hanging right there. With the keys to all their other properties."

"Not about the keys," Meryl propped her elbow on the table. "I mean staying the night. In the house. Where that—that *stranger* died."

"You mean the vagrant?"

The word, in Viola's lettuce-filled mouth with white cream at the corners, sounded both vulgar and elegant all at once. Strange, mostly.

*Vagrant.* Meryl eyed her aunt. "What if it's bad?"

"I'm sure it is."

"There could be needles in there," Meryl pointed out. She wasn't one to mind the more indelicate bits of life. But there was a difference between minding them and sleeping amongst them.

Viola licked the corners of her lips and took a swig of wine. "I'll try not to lie directly on them."

"Let's get a motel room. It'll give us a chance to inspect the place."

"Let's?" Viola asked, taking another swig and swishing this one in her mouth. "You're leaving. Summer vacation. All that."

Meryl pursed her lips. "I'll stay the night."

"Curious?"

"Worried."

"You don't strike me as the worrying type." Viola flicked her fingers up for the bill.

"I've already lost my folks. And now I've done an ID on a dead homeless woman. I'm not going to drive back down here to ID your corpse, too. It'd put me over the edge."

And just like that, Meryl was staying in Gull's Landing. But only for one night.

## CHAPTER 9—DELIA

Bryant had given Delia a week to make arrangements.

She was now forbidden from even calling Bryant—not that she knew where he was staying. Could be with his parents. Could be with... *her*. Any correspondence went through his lawyer. And without one of her own, she felt pitiful and pathetic. Particularly when *Bryant's* attorney assured her that she had more than a week after all. That Bryant would be happy to extend his request should she require more time.

That was the moment Delia knew she'd better find representation of her own. She had no intentions of being a charity case. Even though that's exactly what she was.

Nancy knew an attorney—of course she did. Bill. A friend of Betsy's. A friend of a friend of a friend. Wasn't that always how it went in personal crises? You searched high and low until someone in your circle had someone in their circle who had someone in their circle who could take on a *charity case*.

Thank God for Bill.

He was easy to work with. Compassionate. Kind. The whole shebang. Still, there was nothing he could do about finding Delia lodgings. Not in a week or in a month. He was just her lawyer. Not her mom.

Being as close as she was to Nancy, though, Delia expected an invitation. And it came.

Sunday morning, directly after church, Nancy and Katherine appeared on her doorstep. Or, rather, *Bryant's* doorstep. Incredible how the mind shifted into the new normal so quickly. Delia had already begun to recognize the house and its possessions as belonging to someone else. Someone she was meant to despise. Her *ex*-husband. Soon-to-be, at least.

The humiliating thing? She didn't even hate him. But then, when Delia stopped to think about it, maybe the fact that she wasn't furious—that she wasn't out-of-her-mind deranged about the divorce—meant she had never loved him.

In the paperwork, he cited irreconcilable differences as the reason he couldn't be with her.

Delia wasn't sure if he couldn't reconcile the fact that Delia would never get pregnant—their primary "difference"—or if he just assumed *she* wouldn't reconcile the fact that he was sleeping with another woman. He'd be right. Delia was no doormat.

She didn't care about him *that* much.

Even without the anger. Without the pain. The plain

and simple truth was that Delia had never *truly* loved Bryant to begin with.

She loved what they might have had. The perfection. The life. The *things*. Turned out, none of that was enough. Never would have been.

"Come stay with us," Nancy commanded, snapping Delia out of her musings. She wore a silk headscarf as if it were still the 1950s. Katherine wore one, too, though she looked annoyed beneath it.

"I can't," Delia replied. "I can't do that to you two." She tried for a smile, but when her face broke in two, Nancy pushed past her and into the house.

"You'll stay with me or you'll allow me to find a place for you," she said, then snapped her fingers at her daughter. "Katherine, come along. Make us some hot tea." Nancy took total control, guiding her daughter into the kitchen and fussing in the pantry for teabags.

Delia followed along lamely, slumping into one of the chairs at the kitchen table, which was littered in half-full boxes.

Nancy spied the tea kettle in one of the boxes and withdrew it, passing it to her daughter before turning her attention back onto Delia. "Do you have a copy of the news?"

"The *Gazette*?" Delia asked tearfully, dragging her knuckles beneath her eyes. "No."

"Not that. I mean the *News. News from The Landing*."

"Oh," Delia answered dumbly. "Um." She frowned and thought. Yes. Yes, she probably did. Somewhere. *News from The Landing* was the neighborhood periodical. A pretentious, silly thing with happenings around the block and events to be hosted at the clubhouse. It came out bimonthly, landing squarely on her front porch with the real newspaper, tagging along uselessly.

Delia lifted herself from her seat and glanced across the kitchen.

"Is this it?" Katherine asked, dipping a hand into a box next to the sink.

Nancy reached for it as Delia explained herself. "Packing paper."

"You've made a lot of progress for such a short amount of time," Nancy pointed out.

"I didn't sleep. I'm not sure what to leave. What to take."

"Okay, here," Nancy said, flying back to Delia at the kitchen table and shoving aside a box, ignoring Delia's hopelessness. She smoothed open the glorified brochure on the empty space of table in front of Delia, drawing her finger across the pages until it stopped right where Delia's eyes had already landed.

The Marina Market.

*News from The Landing*'s silly name for their own local classifieds.

"Hmm." Nancy drummed her free fingers on her lips as they both gazed down. After just a few moments, she lowered into the seat beside Delia and shifted the paper more squarely in front of herself. "Let me just look here." A few more murmurs and then, "Ah ha!"

Nancy swiveled the page to Delia and tapped a small square box. "Look there."

"Two bedrooms, one bath. Eighteen-hundred square feet." Delia nodded, flicking her eyes back across the tiny list. "Eighty-thousand dollars?" Delia looked up. "It's for *sale*," she pointed out dumbly.

"Well, yes," Nancy said. "*All* these listings are homes for sale." She waved a hand across the page.

"Nancy," Delia dropped her voice. Feeling awkward and ashamed now, she wasn't sure if she ought to placate her friend and say she'd call. *It'll be fine*. Something like that. Or if she ought to tell the truth.

Trying for comfortably noncommittal, she replied, "Are there any for lease? I'd hate to rush into a purchase."

Delia braced for a laugh or scornful huff. But Nancy just cocked her head. "Don't you want to stay here? In The Landing?"

"Yes," Delia replied meagerly. She did, too. Even if Bryant would still be here, Delia's best friend lived here. Her life was here. He'd have to share the country club with her. He just would.

Nancy dropped her chin and looked at Delia very seriously. So seriously, in fact, that Delia wondered where she'd misstepped. What she'd said wrong.

"Delia," Nancy scolded, her voice solemn, a twinge of concern painting her name. "There are no… *rentals* in *The Landing*."

## CHAPTER 10—MERYL

Meryl parked her car along the street in front of 12 Mill River Road.

Viola would be another fifteen minutes at least. She was stopping at the market to pick up a few cleaning supplies for them, and she said Meryl ought to go along without her.

Now that she was here, though, Meryl wasn't entirely easy with the idea of exploring the just-recently-undeemed crime scene. To be fair, though, the police had never really considered it a crime scene. The weak attempt at crime scene tape strung across the front fence was more to keep out looky-loos than to officially identify the place as a spot of criminal activity.

Once Viola and Meryl had confirmed that they didn't recognize the woman, and after the other three—the chief, the embalmer, and the funeral director—had reiterated amongst themselves that the woman was, indeed, a vagrant, the case had snapped shut.

It made Meryl feel a little sad, in truth. What little

mystery had surrounded the woman's death was swept out with a few pinkening maple leaves, crunchable and valueless. Nothing like they would have been at the start of autumn—signs of change and hope for the future. Now, just relics of the last season. Useless. Nuisances.

The sun had begun her descent behind the house, angling her rays down toward Mill River, which Meryl knew flowed through the forest beyond, but which she couldn't see.

She closed her car door and strode up to the fence on the inside of the craggy walk, and there she stood. And listened. And looked.

Warm, early-evening air greeted her, but the weather felt a little different there, so close to the woods and so far from the ocean. Not warmer or colder. Dryer, perhaps. Like fall was nipping at her heels the farther in she moved from the Atlantic.

A soft, distant gurgling became apparent. Like a babbling brook. Of course, it could have been the wind through the trees. It could have been a neighbor's vanity fountain. It could have been anything, but when Meryl looked left and right, she was reminded that there really weren't any neighbors. At this edge of Gull's Landing, she was officially in the country. A reminder of how sprawling such a small town could be. In square acreage, at least. Or mileage, as the case may be.

Meryl forced herself to focus on the imposing shape before her. The Mill River house was big. Too big. Too big for a country house or a city house or any sort of house that her mother's father should have ever owned.

Gladys Preston's parents had both died when Meryl

was just a young girl—too young to remember them even though her mother swore they attended her fifth birthday party. Even though there were photographs of them in the Prestons' current home in Newark.

PopPop Stevers had been a fisherman, and MomMom Stevers an innkeeper, according to local lore and reaffirmed by Meryl's understanding from her mother. They'd let the house to those souls who sort of wove their ways through small towns. Tourists and, sometimes, traveling salesmen. Bored spinsters on weekend trips with their girlfriends. Itinerants. Whoever had a little change to spare and needed a soft place to land for a night or two. Whether for pleasure or business or sometimes even—according to Gladys—*survival*.

It was any wonder Gladys had kept the place at all. Her siblings, who'd been much older than she and had wandered their own ways across the country, hadn't any interest or sentimental ties to the house. Gladys, apparently, had. Despite the fact that it was a house that never felt like a home, she'd kept it. Didn't do much with it, though, if Meryl's vantage point from the front walk was at all trustworthy. And the fact that a homeless woman had died there.

She eyed the building carefully, accepting that this was the only chance she'd have to see it fresh and new—or at least, new to her. Fresh, well, there was little that could be considered fresh about the place. The stone exterior had a crumbly effect to it, worn at the corners and beneath the eaves. Eaves which gave way to a charming roofline—complete with four gables, it would appear.

Meryl counted the windows under her breath. From the front facade alone, there were eight. Who knew how many stretched across the sides and back?

She raked her hand through her blonde hair, tugging it back across her widow's peak and out of her face before she crossed her arms and continued her examination.

Weathered wooden shutters sagged along the front windows, giving the place a sort of weary look. Beneath one of the windows there had been a little flower box, or what appeared to be a flower box. Dusty weeds sprouted from its surface.

Meryl took a step back from the worn white picket fence that stretched the width of the front and cut at square angles towards the back of the house. Within it, as though trapped, grew long blades of gray grass across two levels of front yard. A lower lawn and an upper lawn were evident, split apart by a set of stone steps, out from which spread tangled bushes. In all, according to Viola and the Prestons' lawyer, the property spanned an entire acre. This was quite something for Gull's Landing. To own an acre of land could make a person royalty. And yet, the Stevers hadn't been royalty. Neither were the Prestons, upon their ownership of the home.

And if this place—12 Mill River Road—was meant to be a castle, then Meryl figured it to be one of those abandoned, crumbling castles, where you might find a sleeping princess. Where an obsessive dragon might snake around the perimeter protecting the fortress like a guardian of virtue.

She looked back over her shoulder, ascertaining that Viola hadn't yet materialized, then stepped back up to the picket fence and reached to open the gate. It fell open, quite literally. The top right corner—where the gate was attached by way of a hinge onto the fence—cracked and snapped away, and the fence fell open, crunching into an old pile of never-bagged pine needles and leaves from years past.

Meryl frowned at it but moved on, making her way over the bramble-buried stone path and up to the house.

The nearer she grew to it, the bigger the house became. Soon, it was clear to Meryl that the stead itself was situated smack dab in the center of the acre property. Too perfectly, almost. Then again, nothing was perfect here, at the back of Gull's Landing where the forest encroached on the seaside town with heavy, thick foliage more appropriate for an off-the-beaten-path heartland than a chic, waterfront locale.

Gull's Landing wasn't chic, of course. It was... homey. Quaint. Cutesy and precious and all the things that bigger Atlantic seaboard communities tried not to be. Sure, it had its stylish enclaves—a boutique here and a neighborhood there. But Mill River Road was *not* one of them.

She made her way up to the front door, the key Viola had secured clutched in Meryl's slick-with-sweat palm. Maybe she ought to wait for her aunt. What if there was a second dead person inside?

Another flutter of yellow tape hung limply alongside the front door, torn down, apparently. Though by man, or beast, or elements, Meryl wasn't sure. She shivered despite the warm air, then plucked the threatening plastic off the door frame and wrapped it around her hand like she was a boxer preparing for a fight. Then, gathering herself momentarily, she thrust the key into the door and pushed into the house.

It wasn't that bad.

Not as bad as she'd imagined.

For starters, the place didn't smell like death. Not like they'd said. Not like the jogger whose dog had taken off for the house had said. Instead, it smelled like life. Like mildew and musty wood and a burnt-out fire and boiling soup, perhaps.

And Meryl could see why. For being abandoned, the house was distinctly... *lived* in.

She had to juggle thinking of the house as the various things it had been. Her ancestral home, namely. An inn, of sorts. Her mother's home—the place where Gladys took her first steps. And then, once the Stevers children left and MomMom and PopPop Stevers died, the house turned into nothing. And then, much later, after Gladys had found other, more important causes, it became a shelter for a no-name woman who'd earned a no-name marker in the back of the new cemetery in town.

The front hall was a cramped, wooden cavern—steps leading upstairs immediately in front of her.

She walked to the staircase, pausing at the bannister. Below and to the left of the stairs, she noticed a door, like a little access point to some other world. Meryl opened it to see that the space was nothing more than a nook, bricked in. The space looked different than the rest of the house, and she wondered if it had once been something more than a utility closet. Maybe a secret room, like a library. Something magical. Her gaze lingered on the deep red bricks, so different from the rest of the wooden house. She closed the door.

At the end of the hall, there appeared to be a kitchen. To the right, a parlor with a fireplace. Elsewhere, probably more dark hollows.

She went first to the parlor, finding a blackened fireplace and a pile of poorly shorn branches, twigs, and even a few newspapers waiting neatly on the hearth. A folded stack of dingy blankets leaned in the corner, near the window. A second small stack of blankets, this one with a worn center, on one of the ornate, turn-of-the-century sofas. Like a little Victorian nest. Meryl frowned and left the parlor for the front hall again.

From that starting point, she walked back to the kitchen.

Moving through the place just as the vagrant woman might have, Meryl couldn't help but think about how the woman had died. She might have had a heart attack. Or a stroke. Or some catastrophic event which took hold of her body and crumpled her to the floor, there in a house that wasn't hers, in a town full of people who didn't know her name.

## CHAPTER 11—LUCY

Marcia and her husband, Chris, were upstairs packing. Fiona and Lucy waited downstairs together in the rocking chair. *I Dream of Jeannie* played on the console television set across from her. Though Fiona was normally this useless, Lucy wasn't.

She was protesting.

"And these?" Marcia stood in the doorway to the living room. She held up a pair of galoshes, navy blue and spotless save for the dust that had accumulated on top of the toes.

"Keep," Lucy muttered, pushing back into a fresh round of rocking as she petted Fiona. Fiona, who stretched pompously across her lap. For the first time in her cat life, Fiona's ire was justifiable. At least, according to Lucy it was.

"Mom," Marcia groaned. "Galoshes?"

"For gardening," Lucy answered. "Keeps the mud at bay."

"And you still garden?" Marcia's voice dropped into a tone of cynicism.

Lucy ignored her, fiddling with the remote until the volume magically raised. Fiona purred loudly, and Marcia sighed and left, the rubber clogs dangling limply from her hand.

It had been three days since Marcia and Scott had arrived to start packing up the house and preparing it for sale. The whole thing—listing the house and moving out—was against Lucy's wishes but *with* her legal permission. She had signed on with the realtor. She had crossed her arms and given one jerking nod of her head.

That afternoon, they were due at Golden Oaks for a tour. Lucy was highly suspicious about this. Did the types who moved into Golden Oaks usually take a tour? If so, how? Theirs wasn't a particularly active clientele. Did they provide golf carts and wheelchairs? Was there a conveyor belt that would carry her through a plate-glass display of miniatures representing the home? *And here is the cafeteria—tapioca and clam chowder! And here is the infirmary, where our residents usually recover...*

That was another thing about Golden Oaks. They called the oldsters who moved in "residents." As *if*, Lucy wanted to say, in echo of a popular phrase she'd heard on TV. *Residents*. More like wards. Wards of Golden Oaks Old Folks' Home.

*Harumph.*

Marcia and Chris suddenly reappeared in front of Lucy, and it occurred to her that she might have drifted off. She had that foggy feeling that a bit of time had slipped away without her realization.

"Mom," Marcia said, hands on hips. "Time to go now."

"Go?" Lucy yawned and went to pet Fiona, who wasn't there. Her lap chilly, she figured she *had* fallen asleep. "What time is it?" What she wanted to ask was, *what day is it?*

"It's after one. We need to be there by one thirty, and we'd better not be late."

"Why not?" Lucy grumbled, accepting Marcia's help up from the rocker.

"Because space is limited at Golden Oaks. We need to make a good impression, Mom." Marcia was patronizing Lucy, and she didn't appreciate it.

Soon enough, they were in the car and on the road. Marcia, having not lived in Gull's Landing since she was eighteen, needed Chris's help to navigate. They ignored Lucy's directions to turn here and there, either because they didn't trust that she knew her way or because they didn't trust that she'd be truthful. The latter was truer.

Marcia drove down Second Street, half admiring the sentimentality of being back in her hometown and half irritated about changes she noticed.

"I thought they opened a new cemetery," she noted, as they rolled past Second Street Mortuary and its accompanying graveyard.

Lucy shrugged in the passenger seat. "What do you think they're gonna do? Bulldoze the old one?"

"Oh, that reminds me, Mom," Marcia went on, ignoring her mother's wry remark. "The woman they found in that house—did you read about that?"

"Mm," Lucy murmured noncommittally.

"You didn't know her, I take it?" Marcia pressed.

Lucy frowned. "Know her? How could I? She was a vagabond."

"Poor thing," Marcia cooed. "How awful."

"She wasn't murdered," Lucy pointed out.

"And how do you know? The article I read was pretty vague. They even opened an investigation."

Lucy pursed her lips. "And now it's closed. Natural causes. Had a service and everything."

"A service? A *funeral* service?" Marcia asked, evidently aghast.

"Buried her out in the old potter's field. That's what they always do," Lucy answered, folding her arms over her chest.

"She had no friends?" Marcia asked. "No one at all?"

Lucy saw clearly where this was going. Her daughter was guilt-tripping her. Borderline threatening her, too. "Some people like it that way, you know," she pointed out.

"Like being alone?"

"Maybe she had a pet."

"She was a homeless woman, Mom."

"Homeless people have pets, all the time. Probably more often than regular people, in my estimation."

"We're here," Chris called from the back seat, his finger poking through the two front seats to point directly in front of them.

And so they were. Just ahead stood a pair of tall, green-leaved oaks swaying in the morning breeze high above a wrought iron gate. The gate, itself, was open.

"How pretentious," Lucy huffed.

"What's pretentious, Mom?"

"They have a gate but it's open. What's the point?"

"Maybe they lock it at certain times," Marcia tried, squeezing her mother's stockinged knee. It was meant as a reassuring squeeze, no doubt, but it came across like a punishment, and Lucy immediately recalled the days of yore. Days when she didn't hesitate to slap her daughter's cheek or swat her backside for being smart. Lucy wanted to do that now. Oh, how the tables could turn.

Marcia drove them through the gates and down a tree-lined drive to a newish building with lots of windows and stucco and everything that Lucy hated in new-fad architecture. Beige paint. Neatly trimmed hedges. Sparse to the max.

The entrance echoed the boring exterior, too, acting like a transition from the outside world into the visitor-friendly lobby. All handrails and ramps. Easy-access *this* and rubber mats *that*.

"Welcome to Golden Oaks," a man greeted them in a set of generic blue scrubs. "How can I help you?"

Marcia nudged Lucy, who gripped the Formica counter and wondered what Fiona was up to. She scowled as subtly as possible.

"We're here for the tour," Marcia answered on their behalf. "Lucy Spaur."

"Ah, yes," he agreed, nodding and plucking a clipboard from his desk. "If you'll just complete this paperwork, I'll go fetch our business manager."

Marcia took the clipboard, and she and Chris moved to the plastic seats in the scant waiting area.

Lucy trudged in their direction, spying a newspaper

on a side table. She grabbed it and set about distracting herself with the classifieds.

That's when Chris cleared his throat and murmured low enough that Lucy wasn't sure he'd said it all. "You know, Lucy, you could just move in with us, if you prefer."

Lucy licked her lips and tasted lipstick. Remnants of the life she wanted to lead. The life of a woman who wore lipstick and slipped into galoshes to do a little gardening and didn't depend on a walker or a cane or even a cat to keep her sane. A woman who was still *alive. Free.*

## CHAPTER 12—MERYL

Meryl felt herself grow sad all of a sudden. She could picture the poor woman. Her eyes closed, like she was asleep. Her skin gray and sunken like she'd been hungry for a long, long time. Meryl shuddered.

She now stood in one of the first-floor bedrooms, the wooden floor a bit soft beneath her feet. A barren space, generally, save for an old full-size iron bed, complete with a crusty quilt.

In the corner of the room, a fireplace. Upon the hearth, a line of little cloth dolls. Meryl could picture a girl playing there, dancing the dolls together as she tugged at a skirt her mother had sewn. To think of the girl as Meryl's own family felt odd. Wrong, even.

The floor in front of the fireplace was darker than the surrounding wooden planks, though that could have been because of foot traffic and its position close to the hearth.

Briefly, Meryl wondered if this might have been a spot

favored by the vagrant woman. Could it have even been, God forbid, her *death spot*?

Surely not.

But then, *maybe*.

The absence of any lingering bad smell throughout the house indicated to Meryl that either the police or their associates had cleaned up or the (albeit brief) passage of time was enough for the foulness of decomposition to fade.

Meryl crouched down to the spot and looked hard. The wood was not only darker, but *different*, too. Newer? In such a short span of time? It made little sense.

Maybe, instead of new wood, there had just been a rug there, damp and trodden so much that it both kept the wood and aged it.

Of course, there had been a rug there. It made perfect sense. The squareness to the dark spot indicated as much. A large, square rug. It was odd to think of such a simple carpet turning into something far ghastlier.

*A soft place to fall.*

Yes, a rug.

She left the room and went to the back of the house, to the kitchen.

She looked around the room, at the potbelly stove in the center of the room, the white farmhouse sink, and white, dated fridge. The wooden counters and exposed cupboards. A single plastic cup and a glass plate sat at the side of the sink.

Meryl opened the back door, then the screen, and made her way onto the back deck.

Sure enough, beyond the wooden porch, which

sagged heavily into the earth, there sat a rolled-up rug. Heavy-looking, dank, and buzzing with hovering insects. So much for crime scene clean-up. It lay in the overgrown grass just feet away from the house, less like a magic carpet and much more like a death shroud.

She didn't go near it. Instead, she turned to go into the house and left the back door open wide. She opened the kitchen windows, too. Just in case there *was* a smell, but that smell was masked by Meryl's morbid fascination with the place and by general, unshakeable grief.

Then, she looped back to the staircase and climbed up, the boards creaking loudly with every step.

On the second landing, Meryl discovered just what the house would have been like in its prime. The second floor boasted furniture and trinkets galore. Even dust-layered and masked by the growing shadows, there was a familiarity to the place. As though perhaps Meryl had been there as a young girl. Maybe she'd come for a weekend once, as a three-year-old. Too young to remember but too old to forget all the way. Maybe the place sort of lived in Meryl.

It wasn't until she entered the first room, however, that her feelings about being there started to truly shift.

Curiosity seized her as she found a photo album sitting on the edge of the nightstand.

The bed next to it, made. Not slept in, though. Or, if it had been slept in, it was so carefully tended to that Meryl would never know.

She pressed a hand to the bed then lifted it and quickly drew it back down, giving the quilt a hard smack. No dust lifted off.

This was where the woman had slept, then. Until her dying day, no doubt, taking good care to make it up after herself. To leave no trace. Sadness swelled in Meryl's gut, but she flipped open the photo album, hoping for fast reprieve.

The first pages were old images. Images of an irritable-looking woman sitting in a gray, floral caftan, in a wheelchair, and staring at something in the distance in the world of the photo. The second, an older man. Standing with a cane, a wry smile driving deep lines into his face. Coke-bottle glasses mottling his eyes from her view.

In the third photo, a row of children, dressed in black and white—or maybe colors, hard to say— each with a look of mischief plastered across his or her face.

In the center of the row, plain as day, young and silly and dirty-faced: Gladys Stevers.

Meryl's stomach cramped and her heart raced. Heat flushed her neck. She flapped the album closed, stepping backwards away from the bed and out of the room, turning to head back downstairs. A crack sounded from below.

"Meryl?"

She pressed a hand to her chest. "Viola," she called from the landing. "I'm up here."

"Come on and help me, wouldya?"

Meryl took the stairs down and joined her aunt at her car, where they unloaded paper bags brimming with cleaning bottles and sponges and washrags. Also in the back, a vacuum and a broom alongside a heavy suitcase.

"Moving in?" Meryl asked.

"For the night. Tomorrow morning, I'm off to the city, and she's all yours."

"You said you'd handle the sale," Meryl pointed out as they re-entered the house.

Viola's gaze drifted up the height of the place. "From afar. As much as I'd like to, I can't stick around town. Work to do. We'll whip this place into shape."

"In a day?" Meryl asked, skeptical.

"What we don't finish, we don't finish."

Meryl didn't like that attitude. But she understood it. She wasn't one to leave much unfinished in life. That was why she'd recently taken to saying "no" to so much. It allowed her to finish what she needed to. Didn't even have to start what she didn't need to. Still, there was only so much time in the day, and Viola had other work, Meryl couldn't protest that.

"And you're sure you can manage the… the *sale*?" Meryl pressed as they made their way inside.

"'Course I can. I'm handling everything else."

The tone didn't escape Meryl. Her aunt was submitting an accusation. A judgment.

Perhaps she deserved it.

The image of the tidy bed upstairs and that of the photograph album on the nightstand glowed to life in Meryl's brain. She ran the back of her hand across her temple, clearing a fresh line of sweat and then tugging her hair into a rubber band as she crossed the threshold behind her aunt.

Viola wobbled into the room, and she looked old. Older than she'd ever looked to Meryl. Too old.

"You know what?" Meryl asked once they set down their bags.

Viola propped her hands on her hips, wincing briefly. "What?"

"I think I can do it."

"Do what?" Viola studied Meryl hard, like she was looking into her niece's soul to assess the honest-to-God truth.

"I'll stay the week. Get it all ready. You've got your job. I have summer."

Viola narrowed her eyes into slits. "Why?"

A small laugh erupted from Meryl. "Because she's my mom. And, well... I need to." The laugh turned quickly to a sob. And that was enough. Enough to prove to Viola that it *was* the truth: Meryl Preston *needed* to stick around 12 Mill River Road. At least for a little while. At least to make things right.

## CHAPTER 13—DELIA

Delia quickly came to learn that Nancy was right. There were no rentals in The Landing. There were hardly any rentals in all of Gull's Landing. At least, not the type Delia could afford. And the types she could afford weren't the type she wanted at all. Yes, Bryant was sending her off with a little pocket change. Yes, she could fight for more, but that would come later. And she needed something now. Something that would get her away from the house she'd called home. Away from *him* and anything to do with him.

It had been a full week since receiving the crushing news, and Delia was effectively out of time. She could move in with Nancy after all, which she'd hate to do—it was embarrassing. Awkward. And there was no end in sight to her need for charity. Or she could lug her bags to a motel and make do. Saturday morning, with her car packed and her key resting beneath the mat as per Bryant's request, Delia plucked the newspaper off the front stoop and left.

For good.

She just wasn't sure where she was going.

Her stomach gurgled in hunger. She'd hardly eaten anything in seven days. Even with her new lawyer's help, she'd spent the week dreading her future. She could have had much longer than a week in the house on Albatross Avenue. But she did not want to be there. Not a moment longer.

Receiving Bryant's note had been the sort of slap in the face from which a woman couldn't recover. It was like a turning point. The plan was set. There was no turning back. Delia could in no way stomach another night spent there, restlessly tossing on the couch, wondering where Bryant was sleeping. With *whom* he was sleeping.

She wanted out *now*, even if it meant she would become something of a transient. Her pride was too great.

Before deciding whether to go to Nancy's or to The Beachside Inn—a frumpy twelve-room roadhouse on the southern edge of town, straddling the line between Gull's Landing and no man's land—she drove to Maeve's. She needed a coffee. Strong. And maybe a danish. Sweet.

"Have a seat where you can find one!" Maeve called out to her as she opened the front door of the eatery and tugged her sunglasses down her nose.

The place was packed. Go figure. A pretty summer Saturday like this one? If anyone questioned whether Gull's Landing was anything short of a bustling boardwalk tourist trap, Maeve's could always prove him or her wrong. Particularly on a gorgeous morning such as this.

Delia's chest rose and fell in a sigh as she scanned the inside. Every table was teeming with tanned breakfast-going families and groups. The bar was lined with singletons—mostly men in golf attire or beachwear, old-timey on their stools with their newspapers framing their silhouettes and cigarette smoke curling in gray tendrils above their heads. She squinted through the windows to the small patio space at the outside corner of the cafe. Two big groups took up more than three quarters of the seating area there, but a small table appeared empty from her vantage point.

She grabbed a plastic menu from the hostess stand and made her way through the secondary door onto the patio, pulling up at the corner bistro set in time to see that she was wrong.

A red-and-white-striped umbrella, tilted against the sunrise, had hidden a lone patroness, sipping her coffee and studying a menu. The woman looked up at Delia. Straw-yellow hair, longish and free, lifting in the breeze. Her heart-shaped face cocked from behind sleek black Ray Bans. Simple but classy. She smiled at Delia. "Hi?" It came out like a question, though not rude. Just... confused. Curious. Interested.

"I'm sorry." Delia flushed. "I didn't see you sitting here. I thought the table was open and—"

"Well, that seat is," the woman answered pointing at the chair across from her. "I'm here alone. Feel free to join me."

Awkward at the exchange, Delia knew she would make it even more awkward by either declining the invitation or accepting it. There was no right way to proceed. Anyway, she had nowhere to go.

"Oh, um." She swallowed and shifted her handbag to

her other arm, the menu getting tangled in the handles as Maeve herself came in behind Delia.

"Coffee, hon?"

Maeve didn't know Delia's name, but she knew Delia. Just as Delia knew that the woman with fire-red hair and lips to match was Maeve. "Okay," she whispered; it was too late to leave now. She plopped into the chair. "I'm terribly sorry," she gushed to the stranger at the table. "This is—*odd*."

"Nah." The woman waved her off. "I could use a little company after the week I've had."

Delia nodded as if she understood. Which she surely did. "Me too," she agreed, a smile cracking across her lips. She pressed her hand to her heart. "I'm Delia. Delia Astor. Well—I used to be Delia Astor. I suppose I'm about to be Delia Fumple again."

The woman, mid-drink, eyed her.

"Sorry. I'm oversharing. Divorce. It was sudden." Delia dipped her chin and silently cursed herself for opening her big, fat mouth.

"Ah, I see. I'm Meryl. Meryl Preston. I don't think that will change any time soon, though," she answered, holding out a broad hand. "Good to meet you."

They shook, and Delia pressed her lips into a line. "Happily married, I take it?"

"Happy, yes. Married, no."

"Happy on the heels of a rough week?" Delia shouldn't pry. She really shouldn't.

The woman lowered her coffee all the way to the table and clasped her hands over her knee. Delia took in her outfit for the first time. Threadbare jeans, washed white and thin. A white t-shirt, clean and crisp. An easy look about her, like she could be wearing a million bucks or nothing. Delia envied her instantly.

"Something like that," Meryl replied mystically. "You here on vacation?"

"Me?" Delia raised her eyebrows. She hadn't often been mistaken for a Shoobie. She used to like it when she was, though. It gave her a chance to correct someone. To spout off that *no, no*. She lived *inland*. In the country club. Like it was its own town within a town. Nicer. Cleaner. Pricier, too. Still local and wise, always wise after a Wildwood upbringing. But polished now. Put together. "I live in town." She frowned. Delia didn't know everyone in Gull's Landing, but she sensed Meryl wasn't a local. "You?"

"Newark. I'm here on... business. I'm fixing up a family house. Getting it ready for sale."

"Oh?"

Maeve returned with coffee for Delia and took both women's orders. When she'd gone again, Delia went on. "Whereabouts is the house?"

Meryl sort of chuckled. "I forget about small towns. Everyone knows everyone. And every*where*, I suppose."

Delia shrugged. Warmth coalesced in her stomach. A combination of the hot drink, surge of caffeine, and friendly banter that had absolutely nothing to do with Bryant or The Landing or anything that mattered. It was... *nice*.

"It's on Mill River Road?" Meryl continued, her voice hitching into a question. "Do you know that area? On the very edge of town, I guess."

"Hm." Delia tapped a finger on her lip then remembered that her nail polish was chipping. She quickly lowered her hand, hiding the crack in her veneer. "I know of Mill River Road, sure. Same street as the local girls' school."

"Girls' school?" Meryl asked, making room on the table for her breakfast—a colorful plate of eggs, fruit, bacon, and toast. "How quaint."

Unsure if Meryl was being facetious or sincere, Delia just smiled, slid her mug out of the way, and thanked Maeve as she set a cinnamon roll in front of Delia.

Meryl indicated in the pastry's direction with her fork. "Now *that's* what I should have ordered."

Stabbing a chunk of the gooey treat, Delia didn't think twice about how much fat or sugar she was about to enjoy. Instead, she tried to envision Mill River Road. "Yep, the old orphanage is out that way," she said matter-of-factly.

"Orphanage?" Meryl asked. "Are you sure? The area is pretty rural. Devoid of life, I'd say." She laughed to herself. "But there are a few other houses on the street. Big ones. Very big. Too big to be houses, really."

"Your mother's house—it's big?" Delia asked, happy to continue the thread of the conversation. As if something was tugging her to it.

"Yep. That's why I'm still here, actually. My aunt and I were going to tidy it up last weekend, but that was a crazy notion. Turns out it needs a lot of work, and I have the extra time, so..." Meryl shrugged.

"Oh, right. No husband," Delia remarked between bites. It wasn't meant as a slight. Just... an observation. A reason the woman would have so much free time. Then she frowned. "Do you work?"

"I'm a teacher. Seventh grade math."

"Did you get time off to stay here, or—"

"Summer vacation," Meryl answered, swallowing a bite of eggs and washing it down with a hearty gulp of coffee.

Delia nodded. "Will you stay all summer then? Since you have accommodations." The word stung her lips as it passed through. "Will you need any—*help*?"

Meryl eyed her. "I wasn't planning on staying all summer, no. But I guess I'd have to if I don't find some help. It's quite a project, that place. Totally abandoned. In disrepair." She lowered her mug. "Why? Are you in the market?"

## CHAPTER 14—MERYL

Driving back to the Mill River house, Meryl felt a knot twist up in her stomach. Delia was following her on the short drive into the back hills of town.

Meryl wouldn't have pressed the matter if Delia hadn't been so reluctant. Her decency made all the difference. Made her normal. Made her safe.

Was it weird to strike up a fast friendship? Weird to invite someone into your life after only just meeting them?

Having formed quality friendships so rarely in her life, Meryl wasn't sure. Then again, her parents had done just that. Allowing in veritable strangers to their family Christmases and Thanksgivings and Easters. She was always shifting over a seat or bringing an extra chair to the table. All growing up, any event was never just a Preston family event. It was a Preston family and friends thing.

She parked her car on the street and popped out,

shielding her eyes from the sun to see Delia pull in behind her. An expensive car. Certainly not something befitting a woman who was looking for a place to stay for the night... or the summer...

"Here we are." Meryl waved a hand up.

Delia stretched from the driver's seat and hooked a thumb behind them, the way they'd come. "I was right," she said. "The Shearwater School for Girls."

Meryl cocked her head. "Really?"

Joining her at the picket fence, Delia pointed down the street. "See that little drive there. The clearing?"

Meryl craned her neck and squinted. "I see a mailbox, sure."

"And the little wooden sign beneath it?"

"Oh, yes. I just—I figured it was an address sign or something."

"That's the school. It's a boarding school, in fact. For wayward girls. Orphans. Foster girls, too."

"Leftovers," Meryl murmured, then paled, stealing a guilty glance at Delia. "I'm sorry."

"No, you're right. Leftovers." Delia's face was blank to the point of sadness.

"It must be quite a big property to hide such a place. The land around it, I mean."

"Lots of trees. Lots of places to get lost in, yeah. To hide." Delia cleared her throat and twisted back to the Prestons' house. "Wow. I remember this house."

Frowning, Meryl asked, "Remember it?"

Delia blinked then sucked her lips inside of her teeth. "I spent a year at Shearwater."

"For school?"

"And residence," Delia answered. Meryl thought her nose twitched. "My senior year of high school. After that, I moved to Gull's Landing for good. From Wildwood, I mean. And, here I've stayed. Until now, I suppose." Delia glanced at the ground then squinted back up at Meryl. "Your offer is pretty generous, but like I said—the motel has vacancies."

"Why stay in a motel when you can stay in a decrepit mansion?" Meryl joked. "But seriously, I could use a little help, if you don't mind getting your hands dirty, and it gives you a place to figure things out. Right?"

Delia nodded slowly, twisting the handle of her handbag this way and that. "You don't know me."

"That makes us even," Meryl answered. "And anyway, I don't have much to lose, truth be told. You won't find anything to rob me of. And if you murder me in my sleep, well, that waitress saw us leave together, just keep in mind." Meryl winked at Delia, who flushed but smiled in spite of herself.

"Okay, well—" Delia twisted her foot on the pavement and faced the house. "How is this going to work, exactly? Do you have an application or…"

Meryl considered this, staving off her own laughter. "For renting a room or for working with me?"

"Um." Delia bit down on her lower lip and shrugged her bag back onto her shoulder. "I don't know, Meryl. It's such a nice offer, really. And you—*you* seem so nice. But I can't just…"

"Just what? Rent a room and help me out?" Meryl didn't mean to sound desperate. She *wasn't* desperate.

Just... lonely. And confused. And unsure how in the world she was going to sell 12 Mill River Road.

And not because of its condition. She didn't even need the money, really.

She was unsure because of something tugging at her insides. Something she needed but couldn't quite name. Something to get her through the grief. Something to get her through a summer of nothingness.

*Something.*

## CHAPTER 15—LUCY

After the tour of Golden Oaks and Chris's lukewarm offer to host her, Lucy's life melted into tapioca. Gooey. That's what Lucy thought, at least. A gooey blob of an existence. Formless, save for the saucer of her daughter and son-in-law who were trying desperately to make something of such a bland, feeble dessert. Or, if not *make* something of it, contain it, at least. Save it. Though from what, Lucy wasn't quite sure.

Upon arriving back home, a dramatic argument had broken out. Lucy had asserted herself, telling her daughter and son-in-law that she wouldn't move into an old folks' home and wouldn't stand by—or sit by—as they packed her house and prepared it for the market. They needed to leave.

But that's when catastrophe struck, you see.

Just as Lucy was ushering the cranky pair out of her house, Fiona darted between her legs, and—in a chaotic attempt to save Fiona and herself—Lucy sailed awkwardly through the air, landing hard on the wood flooring.

She was fine, in truth. Only her pride was shaken. But still, back they loaded themselves, into the sedan and down to the hospital. Marcia and Chris ignored the fact that Lucy didn't even need so much as her cane or an extra hand to get in and out of the vehicle.

Harumph.

The doctor disagreed, however. And the x-ray Lucy underwent agreed with the doctor, conveniently.

She had sprained her wrist and now needed a brace. Not only that, but they'd kept her there. *Overnight*, mind you. A whole hospital stay for something as pesky as tripping over Fiona. This, naturally, hadn't helped Fiona's cause; it took all of Lucy's might to convince her daughter to go and check on the poor dear.

By the time Lucy had returned home, Marcia and Chris had effectively moved in for the week, finding themselves to be further committed to getting Lucy "out of this house and somewhere *better*" for her. Hah! As if she needed sponge baths and large print crossword puzzles. Well, she *did* need large print crossword puzzles, to be fair. But Golden Oaks wasn't the only place a woman of a certain age could get hold of guilty pleasures.

And such pleasures were now nearly out of Lucy's reach. Quite literally. With a bum right wrist, she couldn't work the pen into the boxes. Instead, she was relegated to reading the paper, and *that* is precisely when she started to formulate her idea. An idea she couldn't quite execute until she had a private moment.

So, for the time being, she played ailing mother,

cuddling poor, maligned Fiona and watching her soaps while Marcia and Chris spent the week packing.

Yes, Marcia and Chris were packing. Packing and squabbling amongst themselves regarding what to do with it all. It turned out Marcia was a little more sentimental than she'd purported to be, wringing her hands over what to purge, what to store. What to take back to her own home.

Despite Marcia's reluctance, though, she and Chris (with Lucy's bitter consent) put the house on the market midway through the week. And on that note, Lucy was expected to prepare to enter Golden Oaks. No, it was true that Lucy hadn't so much as completed the application for the retirement home, but they had her down as a person of interest—Lucy's words, not theirs. It was far easier to let go of her house than to accept a new one, for some reason. The opposite should have been true. At least, that's how life normally went. You were more hesitant to let go of the past but pretty excited to embrace the future. When you got to be wrinkled and silver and a simple thing such as a staircase was cause for alarm... well, the past ought to have been more difficult to release. But with a future like the one promised to Lucy, there wasn't much to embrace.

When Marcia and Chris didn't press Lucy on completing the application and taking her second tour—what Golden Oaks referred to as the "commitment phase"—Lucy's heart warmed a tad.

She suspected that the lack of a push had something to do with her daughter's hope that Lucy would demand to come live with them—in Ocean City in a comfortable, suburban home the likes of which many a grandmother lived in with her descendants, happily braiding her granddaughter's hair as *The Brady Bunch* blared on the television.

She couldn't picture such a scenario, however. Firstly, Lucy had no granddaughter to speak of. Or grandson, for that matter. Furthermore, there was the question of awkwardness. A grandmother could be a welcome presence in a home with children. She could help with morning routines and dinner preparations, taking her seat in the middle of the table and passing the beans and bread. She could tuck in the unruly child who listened to no one save for ol' Grandmom.

With just Marcia and Chris there, Lucy would be little more than a third wheel. A charity case, for goodness' sake. Lucy Spaur was no charity case. But that wasn't the worst of it. The worst of it was that Chris was allergic to cats. Not too allergic to pack the house, mind you, but allergic enough to convey to Marcia in hushed whispers that if Lucy was going to take them up on their offer of a room, well, then Fiona would have to go.

Lucy found this to be unacceptable. Here she was, her hands tied as her daughter packed her house and listed it for sale as though Lucy was infirm, but she wasn't. Not entirely.

Certainly not too infirm to page through the *Gazette*, landing squarely on the inseam of the Classifieds, where she read a miniature ad that was nothing short of an omen.

*ROOM FOR LET. Homeowner seeking second tenant. ND,*

NS. *Inland home. No dogs. Cats fine. Inquire with Norm. #9816.*

An omen, indeed.

Shuffling sounded from above and Lucy glanced down the hall. The coast was clear. Her telephone sat, unpacked, in its little nook. Fiona slept in her lap.

Quietly and very, very slowly, Lucy removed Fiona, lifting her up and lowering her to the floor. The orange girl scampered away, clearing a path for Lucy.

She made her way to the phone, lowering to the seat nearby. More shuffling above. She paused.

Then, she folded open the classifieds page to the contact number, tucking her free pinky into the dialer and pulling the numbers off until the phone rang.

Soon enough, she was connected with the advertiser.

"Hello?"

"Hello," Lucy replied, "yes. I'm calling in reply to your listing for a tenant. Is this, er—" Lucy quickly glanced at the ad, "Norm?"

"Why, yes. I'm Norm. Norman Grimwood. I posted the ad."

"Is the room still available?" Lucy went on, lowering her voice as the thumping from above seemed to dissipate. It wouldn't do for Marcia to overhear and question her.

"It is," the man on the line answered. Lucy wasn't too keen on a male landlord, particularly if it was his house she'd be sharing. Still, there'd be men at Golden Oaks, wouldn't there? And then there was Chris, naturally. Norman Grimwood was a familiar name, anyway. Lucy didn't ask about it, but she did have one question. A make-or-break-it question.

"And is the room on the first floor of your home, by chance?" she asked, biting her lower lip and squeezing her eyes shut as her hand wobbled on the telephone receiver.

"*Mom!*" a cry came from the top of the stairs. Lucy froze, her hand gripping the telephone harder than ever.

But it didn't much matter. Norman Grimwood replied to her just then. "It's on the second floor, actually."

The air eased from Lucy's mouth like an old balloon that someone had pinched and cut into, wheezing out in struggled breaths. "Thank you anyway," she whispered and cradled the receiver.

"Mom?" Marcia was now at the base of the stairs, a box of stuff in her arms. "You okay? You look sick."

Lucy didn't admit that she *was* sick. She tried for a smile, but her lips were dry and the lower one split. She pressed a fingertip to it, the blood there a reminder of the life she had left. A reminder that there was still fight left in her. That she didn't have to be a burden on her daughter. Or a danger to herself.

"Oh, Mom," Marcia set the box down and, inside, Lucy spied Fiona's spare food dish and a fresh box of litter. "Let me help."

But Lucy batted her away.

"Who were you talking to?" Marcia asked, accepting her mother's resistance and returning to the box.

"No one," Lucy answered. "Never mind. Just do your packing and mind your own business."

Marcia frowned at her, then clicked her tongue and

shook her head. "I hope you're nice to the people at Golden Oaks." With a tilt of her head, Lucy's daughter sashayed out the front door and to the moving van.

And Lucy decided to make a second phone call.

To the same number as before. But this time, instead of redirecting to an advertiser, she told the operator that *she*, Lucille Carrigan Spaur, had an ad to post.

## CHAPTER 16—DELIA

An hour later, Delia's fleeting idea to leave town had dissipated into the warm afternoon like a memory—fading more distant with each room she toured in the Mill River house.

Besides, Gull's Landing was the only home she'd known in years. She was comfortable. People knew her and she knew them. Even if she had to give up the HOA, that didn't mean she had to give up the friendships she'd already formed. Although, only her friendship with Nancy had really mattered so far.

But there, out in the boonies of the town with this effervescent, willful stranger with a knack for deep cleaning and a penchant for small talk… it felt like maybe a new start could still be possible. Even if it was in the same town as ol' Bryant.

Delia had packed everything she wanted into her car. Bryant had indicated that she could take the lot, but Delia preferred to save only her most prized possessions. When it came down to it, it turned out that she had lived in a house full of prizes, but not prized possessions. Nothing of real meaning. Sure, a few high-end clutches. Her heels. Garments and makeup and the accoutrements that would carry her through such a rough spell. But furniture and art mattered little to her. Even less when she figured she wouldn't have a place to put it all.

Now she did have a place to put her things. At least for the summer. But the tour of the house had proved there'd be no room for it, anyway. Not only that, but the decor would be so totally off. All the things that her country club house *was*—postmodern, black-and-white, sleek—this house was *not*.

They stood in the kitchen together. Meryl had just finished scrubbing out the fridge, and Delia had cleaned the countertops, the island, the oven and the stovetop. They were nearly finished in here, and it would give them a place to take a break inside, safe from the heat—but not from the stuffy air of the house.

"How did they cool this place?" Delia asked as she took a long swig of her fountain soda. Meryl had left to fetch them drinks from a convenience store. Snacks, too. Delia wasn't hungry, though.

"I suppose by throwing open the windows. Turning on the fans."

Delia hadn't noticed any fans. She waved her hand in front of herself and pulled her blouse off her chest, forcing air down to her skin. It felt good. She wondered what Nancy would think if she could see her now.

"So," Delia went on, trying for easy conversation, "you think you'll put it up for sale in the fall, then?"

"I think so," Meryl answered. "Although, who

knows?" Her gaze drifted to the window, and the whole of her took on a dream-like quality. Like someone who was searching. Someone who didn't know what she wanted in life.

Someone very opposite of Delia, who knew quite well what she wanted in life.

"If you can afford to keep it, it'd be a nice summer home." Delia didn't dare offer to play property manager. Hopefully, by September, she'd be well on her way to the next phase of her life. Maybe she'd find someone with higher sperm count. Or someone who wanted to adopt. Someone with a little girl of his own, a girl who'd lost her mother in some garish tragedy. Someone who wanted the exact same thing as Delia.

"I can't. I can hardly afford my own condo. Teacher's salary," Meryl replied. "Then again, who knows what'll come from my parents' estate. I'll find out soon, but in the meantime, I plan to make a go of turning a profit here. Not because I need the profit, mind you." She paused for effect. "But because this place deserves a facelift. You know? Anyway, I can't keep it, profit or not. I'm good where I am. In Newark. In my condo. With my seventh graders." She smirked at Delia. "Do I sound like a lonely spinster?"

Delia shook her head. "You sound fulfilled." Now it was Delia's turn to pause. "I think?" Meryl burst into laughter, throwing her head back and her hair with it. Delia chuckled, too. "I'm sorry. I'm not really sure. Losing your folks is hard, though."

"Yours are gone too, eh?" Meryl asked, joining Delia at the wooden kitchen table.

She nodded in reply. "Never met my dad. Mom died when I was in high school. I think she's *gone* gone, if you know what I mean."

"Geez," Meryl answered. "That's awful. I'm so sorry."

"That's life. I've long since moved on. Or, I suppose, I thought I had. Now I'm a little bit back to square one. Mill River Road. All alone again, in some ways."

"No other family? Friends?" Meryl inquired.

"I have one close friend. Nancy. She's a neighbor. Or... *was*. No other family, no. Just me."

"Kids?" Meryl squeezed her eyes shut. "Sorry. I'm prying."

"No, no. It's fine. I wish I did, but no. No kids."

Meryl shifted, her expression inscrutable. "I guess we have that in common, then."

Delia smiled. "For now, at least," she answered, wryly.

"Hey, anything's possible." Meryl winked at Delia, and the deal was done. They were friends. Just like that.

## CHAPTER 17—MERYL

The next morning, Meryl awoke with a start.

Two weeks out from her parents' death, Meryl still struggled with sleep. She was exhausted and haunted.

The best thing would be to return home. Let life settle back in as usual. Why in the world Meryl thought it was smart to stay on in Gull's Landing was beyond her. But now, here she was, playing hostess to a scorned stranger who needed a place to stay and a little work to get by. Meryl found it laughable, really, to be providing such charity under the circumstances.

Groping for her wristwatch on the nightstand, it took her eyes a minute to adjust and see the time. Well before six in the morning.

At least it was after four, though. The previous days had seen Meryl up at the ungodly hour of three-thirty, wired and anxious.

She moved downstairs, careful to tread lightly on the

creaking staircase so as not to wake Delia, who'd claimed one of the three bedrooms on the first floor.

Three more bedrooms took up the second floor. Each floor had its own bath, complete with a claw foot tub and pedestal sink. In addition to the bedrooms were extra rooms. A parlor, serving as the living room; the kitchen; dining room; and a small, first-floor study, its walls lined with shelves full of soggy old books. Meryl had already thumbed through a few volumes, ascertaining that the library was filled vastly with fictional classics and appeared to lack anything personal. No diaries or journals. Nothing to indicate that one of the Stevers had left a piece of herself (or himself) behind.

There had been no coffee maker left behind in the kitchen, so Meryl had picked up a cheapie at Al's Appliances and grabbed filters and grounds at the market, along with easy-to-prep foods like muffins and TV dinners. Turned out the ancient microwave was still in working order, and that had been nothing short of a Godsend. Without a microwave, Meryl might have had to give up entirely. And there was no way she'd have bought one of those. Not for a quick flip.

Of course, she was starting to wonder if her stay at 12 Mill River Road was going to be so quick after all.

"Morning!" The cheery greeting caught Meryl so off guard that she screamed. "I'm sorry!" Delia added behind a small smile. She had appeared from around the corner as Meryl stepped into the kitchen. "I'm so sorry. I figured you knew I was in here and that's why you came. I... I couldn't sleep."

"Me either," Meryl replied. "Although, I slept a little

better than usual, I have to say. I haven't stayed in bed past four AM in two weeks."

"Another commonality between us," Delia answered, offering Meryl a steaming mug of coffee.

"It's a wonder grief doesn't kill more often. Who can survive on so little shuteye, you know?"

"I know. I mean... divorce isn't the same as death, but —" Delia shook her head pitifully.

"It is," Meryl disagreed. "It's the death of a marriage. Of a relationship. I think that's grief-worthy, right? Losing something you had? For good." She flicked at glance at Delia, whose smile had slipped away. Meryl changed the subject. "I think part of my issue is sleeping in a house where someone died. Have you ever done that before?"

"Slept in a house where someone died?" Delia echoed. She frowned, seeming to consider the question seriously, as though she'd slept in many houses and had to comb through the memories of all her wakeful nights. Weeks. Months. *Years*, perhaps. "I'm pretty sure children died at Shearwater before I got there."

Meryl gasped. "You're joking."

Delia shook her head gravely. "It's an old orphanage. Boardinghouse. School. If you think there's history here, you should take a walk up the street. That place was like a crypt for local horrors of the saddest kind. Rough girls. Sick girls. Abandoned girls. And the teacher? Let's just say education was the least of her concerns. I managed to earn my high school diploma simply by surviving that hell-hole."

"Wow." Meryl took a sip of her coffee and lowered

into a chair. Delia had the paper open and was scanning through the pages. "Can I see the classifieds?" she asked.

Delia flipped to the thin section at the back and extracted it from the rest of the paper, handing it over. "Looking for a local teaching job?" she joked.

Meryl snorted. "Actually, I wanted to see what the real estate market is like around here. Get an idea of a listing price."

"So, you're content with your classes up in Newark, then?"

Meryl shrugged. "Sure. Easy enough kids. My condo is nice. Life is good. I'm happy there." As she said it, the skin on the back of her neck prickled and she felt her face flush. As if she was caught in a lie.

Was she?

Quickly, Meryl scanned the little boxes of advertisements. Three-bedrooms were common among the homes for sale in Gull's Landing.

A few two-bedrooms, too. Older, to be sure. Only one bathroom, perhaps.

One listing on First Street sang out to her. A two-story walk-up in its original, historic condition. Three bedrooms, one bath. Well-loved and owned by just one family since its construction at the turn of the century. Meryl wondered who was selling. And... why?

Was it the orphaned daughter of parents who'd cast their attention elsewhere? Was she bitter over something, too?

Was it the residents themselves? Too brittle to care for the property any longer. Ready for something easy.

Something manageable and safe, complete with a first-floor bath and a ramp into the house?

Who knew? Meryl pushed away the stab of guilt and glanced to the next listing.

A four-bedroom caught her attention. Something closer to what Meryl was looking for. More comparable to the sizable Stevers home. "Here's one," she said, clearing her throat and reading aloud. "Beautiful family-sized home in The Landing. This one will go fast! Four ample bedrooms, three lavish baths—all renovated and decorated in tasteful modern decor. Furnishings included in escrow!" Meryl blew out a low whistle. "It even has a little photo. Gorgeous house. And that price tag. Wowee." She tilted the paper toward Delia, who did a double take.

"That's my house," she replied, her jaw falling open as she looked up at Meryl.

"Oh my," Meryl pulled the page away, attempting to save her new friend from herself. "Delia," she continued, "I'm sorry."

Delia's face had gone white, and she'd set her coffee down. "I can't believe it. It's been... *days*."

"Can he do that? Without your permission?"

Delia shrugged. "It's his house. He bought it independently of me. All our finances were separate."

"Separate," Meryl murmured. "Hm."

"Anyway, I'll tell Bill—my lawyer. Maybe I'm owed something, but I won't get my hopes up."

"Do you want it?" Meryl asked.

"The house you mean?" Delia tapped a finger on her lip, its paint chipping in jagged lines down the nail. "I thought I did." Then, surprisingly, she laughed. A mirthless sort of laugh. The kind reserved for villains.

Meryl considered the woman's answer. She wondered if she wasn't in a similar position in her own life. Torn between what she thought she wanted... and what she got. Or, what she *actually* wanted, as the case may be.

"Can I see that?" Delia interrupted her thoughts. Meryl passed her the paper.

"If you're sure."

Delia studied the listing briefly, but Meryl watched her eyes dart about the page, looking elsewhere now. After some moments, Delia clicked her tongue softly. "Aw," she murmured. "How sweet is this?"

Meryl finished the last of her coffee and started into a muffin. "Hm?"

"Look," Delia opened the page to Meryl and pressed a finger down on a tiny box at the very bottom of the final column.

*Elderly Single White Female seeks room for rent and roommate, too! Me: good health, non-smoker, quiet. Can help cook. Prefer first floor. May I bring my cat? #0212*

Something stabbed Meryl about the listing. A sadness. A longing for her mother and father. Her eyes watered and her chest tightened. "Poor thing," she murmured, the words catching in her throat.

"Not sure she needs much pity. Seems pretty independent to me," Delia pointed out. "That's the most adorable little ad I've ever seen. I sure hope she finds someone."

Meryl looked up at Delia, a wild thought seizing her. "Maybe she has."

# CHAPTER 18—LUCY

Lucy's house was a shell of itself. All that was left were the very basics—enough to tide her over for one more week there. Within that week, Marcia told her, Lucy had to make her "own decision."

It really didn't feel much like her "own decision." Her "own decision" would be to stay put. She could sleep in her rocker and never step foot on the second floor. She could use the kitchen sink for her bathroom needs. It'd be fine. She'd make do just fine.

But Lucy knew as well as Marcia that, in reality, it was only a matter of time before she sprained something else or, worse, broke her hip.

That's exactly why she had asked for one week to make up her mind. If she didn't get a call back from an interested roommate in one week, then she'd go to Golden Oaks. Lucy would rather sacrifice her freedom than her dignity; and putting a burden on her daughter and son-in-law would be just that: undignified.

Which is why, when she received a phone call on

Saturday morning, just after her cup of tea, she nearly fainted. It'd been just one day since she'd run her ad.

And now here she was, answering a stranger's phone call.

"I'm calling in regards to your ad in the paper. You're seeking a room to rent?" the warm voice asked.

Lucy's stomach churned with butterflies. "Yes, this is Lucille Spaur. You may call me Lucy."

"Lucy. Hi. My name is Meryl. Meryl Preston. How are you?"

"I'm fine, thanks. How are you, Mary?"

"It's Meryl, actually. M-E-R-Y-L."

Lucy winced and made a face. "Oh, pardon me. I'm sorry. Meryl, is it, then?"

"Meryl, yes. And I'm doing well. I—well, in regards to your ad, you see, I'd like to talk further. I'm not sure I have exactly what you're looking for. But I, well, I have a house, and in this house, I surely have rooms for rent. One of which is currently rented. The circumstances aren't maybe quite right but—"

"I'm very interested," Lucy said immediately, stealing a look at Fiona. "And pets? You accept pets?"

"With a deposit, yes. We can discuss pets," Meryl answered.

Lucy pushed her smile down deep. "There's just one other thing," she said, her voice low now as she fidgeted with the telephone cord.

"Sure," Meryl replied.

"Stairs. Are there—are there many stairs or steps in the house? Is the room you have on the first floor? I'm fine to manage stairs, mind you—it's really nothing more than a preference, you see. I mean that, plus the rent payment—those are just two other questions I have."

"We can discuss the rent payment, of course," Meryl replied. Her voice was butter in Lucy's ear. "As for stairs, yes. But that shouldn't be a problem. We've got two available rooms on the first floor. No other stairs to speak of, save for the front stoop, if you can manage. But it's just two steps. There's a railing."

Lucy envisioned the two steps. They'd be a welcome reprieve. Really, they would.

"That's just wonderful," she gushed, rubbing her fingers together at her knee to summon Fiona.

"As I mentioned, though," Meryl continued, her smooth voice crackling around the edges. "I'll have to tell you a little more about the house and its... circumstances."

A knot took the place of the butterflies, curdling and twisting Lucy's insides in the threat of disappointment. "Circumstances, dear?"

"I think the best thing is for us to meet and talk. You can see the property and your would-be room. We can meet you—my, um, my friend and I, I mean. And we can explain everything."

Lucy shook her head, all too aware of a scam when she heard one. "Oh, I see," Lucy answered stiffly. Fiona curled around her ankles and visions of Golden Oaks flashed through her mind.

"Here, I'll just give you the address, and you can come by anytime. Today or tomorrow would be great. It would help us... make some long term decisions."

Lucy knew she'd be going nowhere. Not only were

her driving days over, but the longer she spoke with Meryl the more she was convinced this was one big sham. She never ought to have put an ad in the paper. How humiliating. Still, her free hand curled around the pencil at her telephone desk, and she hovered it above her pad of paper in time for Meryl to give her the house number and street.

"It's 12 Mill River Road. Do you know the area?"

A crimp formed between Lucy's eyebrows. "Mill River Road, you say?"

"Yes. 12 Mill River Road," Meryl repeated. "I'll be here 'round the clock, mostly. If you'll just give me half an hour advance notice before arriving, I'll be sure to be available to chat."

"That's the—" but by the time her memory had jogged well enough to form a sentence, Lucy thought better of it. No way could she convince Marcia to drive her to the scene of a crime. A biweekly market trip was one thing. This, quite another.

Yet, no way could Lucy resist going. Jessica Fletcher came to mind and Lucy's all-time favorite television program. The circumstances, whatever they may be, had all the makings of a terrific episode of *Murder She Wrote*. It was enough to accept the chances of being scammed.

"I'll be there today," Lucy found herself saying, a disembodied voice drifting across the phone lines into the distant backroads of Gull's Landing. The same road where they found that poor wretch. The same road where Lucy had her very first job. Back when Marcia had started school. Not there, though. Oh no.

The newly acquainted women ended their phone

call. And after, Lucy placed another. To the Gull's Landing taxi-cab service.

"Fiona," Lucy said, tickling beneath the feline's fuzzy white chin, "we might have a way out of this mess after all."

## CHAPTER 19—DELIA

Delia picked at the small remnants of her nail polish, clearing the last bits of her old life away. Although, Delia still felt quite firmly rooted in her old life. So much so that she wasn't entirely comfortable with Meryl's grand plans.

Sure, Delia could commit to three months at 12 Mill River Road. It would save her. Give her the layover she needed on her way to the second phase of her life. On her way to meet the next man who might marry her and whisk her off into a beautiful home with promises of babies in bonnets and Saturday family days at the park. Sundays together on the beach. Winters at a family ski lodge once their little tykes had grown and taken to the slopes with a passion, much like Delia had always longed to.

Meryl's idea was a kind one. A sympathetic one. But it was rushed, too. As rushed as her offer to move Delia into the old house to help get it into market-ready condition.

If Delia didn't know better, she'd think the strong,

blonde woman in her white t-shirts and threadbare jeans wasn't as strong as she seemed to be.

"What are you thinking?" Delia asked Meryl as they thwacked rugs with broom handles off the back porch.

"I'm thinking these might not be salvageable," Meryl replied, swinging her wooden stick firmly into the center of the braided floor covering like a softball player. A millionth round of dust plumes puffed off, drifting on a warm breeze into the woods.

"I mean about this Lucy lady," Delia replied, giving her own rug a thwack. "Should I stop?"

Meryl lowered her broom and ran the back of her hand across her forehead. "For now, sure. And as for Lucy, I don't know. Truthfully. I don't know. Maybe it's a stupid idea."

"What will you say, anyway? That she can rent for three months then move? Or are you considering letting the house beyond the summer? Into the fall and winter? You'll need to have the chimney cleaned. Maybe baseboard heaters? Or is there a working furnace—"

Meryl dropped into a wooden chair at the edge of the porch, her head falling into her palms. "I don't know," she muttered. "I'm sorry about this."

Delia frowned, nervous now. "Sorry? About what?

Meryl waved a hand across the yard. "About inviting you here. Thinking I could make this work. Giving it a chance."

Delia kept quiet. She didn't know Meryl well enough to react appropriately. Sure, they'd become fast friends, but that was on the condition of normal behavior. Not... a mental breakdown. She had no choice, though. The only option was to make this work.

"Meryl," Delia said, her voice serious, "do you think you'll *keep* this place?"

Meryl turned to her, her lips pursed. "Why would I do that?"

"Why else call about the ad? And invite that woman over? I mean, don't get me wrong here, I'm your tenant, too. And if you *do* keep the place… who knows what will happen?" Delia smiled hopefully. There was always the chance things would go inordinately *well*. "But if you don't, she's clearly older. Wouldn't you—"

"Get her hopes up?" Meryl finished Delia's sentence.

"Right," Delia answered, her tone measured.

"Who knows?" Meryl shrugged. "Maybe there's a reason I didn't let good ol' Aunt Viola take over. Maybe this place is calling to me."

"You mean as a rental property?"

"That," Meryl agreed, "or something more."

"With the house nearly clean, what's your next goal?" Delia asked as she followed Meryl back in. The rugs hung stiffly over the porch railing, airing out for who knew how much longer.

Once inside, Meryl poured two glasses of lemonade. "Repairs," she answered between sips. "First the furnace, which is out of order entirely. Then, who knows? Maybe the roof? In the meantime, though, maybe we could tackle the yards."

"I can work a rake," Delia offered. And she could, too. She could work just about any tool or housekeeping device you put in her hands. It had been years since she *had* wielded anything, though. "I could even work a chainsaw if you're really serious."

Meryl snorted through her drink, spraying a bit of lemonade along with her laughter and wiping at her mouth. She gave Delia a hard look. "You don't really add up; you know that?"

Delia flinched, twisting her chin away by mere centimeters, as if she were bracing for a punch to the face. She swallowed and her nostrils flared involuntarily, a habit she'd learned from the ladies in The Landing. The lip pursing and the nose flaring and the chin jutting —all in order to achieve the perfect angles for the face. The perfect *look*. The country club *look*. "I'm not sure what you mean," she answered at last, carefully.

"I mean you—look at you, Delia. You're all class. This entire week, I've waited for you to, I don't know, fall apart or something. Sob, maybe. Lose your mind, even. But no. Each morning, you wake up at the crack of dawn, brew coffee, wear a tidy little working outfit. You use words like *retire* for the evening and *oh, my*. But you went to Shearwater. You can work a chainsaw?" Meryl set down her drink and folded her arms across her chest.

Delia might have given in. Might have revealed that she was a ruse. A facade of the put-together housewife. A fake. But something occurred to her. "I could say the same about you."

Meryl scoffed audibly. "I'm... what you see is what you get with me. For better or worse," she added with a smirk.

But Delia shook her head. "You're beautiful and hardworking. You're a teacher. You loved your parents. You own your condo. No man? No kids? And you're what... thirty-seven?"

"Forty," Meryl replied.

"Where've you been, Meryl?"

The woman stood in front of her, her jaw tensing visibly. "You mean what have I been doing all my adulthood?" She chuckled. "I could say the same about you."

Delia couldn't help but smile at her own words in her new friend's mouth. "I've been living a lie, probably."

"Me too—probably." Meryl smiled warmly.

And then, the doorbell rang.

## CHAPTER 20—MERYL

Meryl didn't have the slightest clue what she was getting herself into. Technically, she was supposed to be back in Newark, recovering from the school year and her parents' death and finding a way to enjoy the first kiss of summer.

Instead, she was lingering in Gull's Landing, hiding. Pretending, even.

In the week she and Delia had lived at the Mill River house, they'd secured not only basic utility services but also a phone line. Meryl's first mistake had been calling Viola to let her know. Ever since, the phone had been all but ringing off the hook. Soon enough, Meryl and Delia both learned to ignore it. Viola's news was limited to minor morsels of the sale of the Prestons' other properties in the hopes of scoring an inkling about "what in the world Meryl was still doing there, in Gull's Landing, where that woman died?"

This from *Viola* of all people. Meryl had invited her

back down for a long weekend at some distant point in the future.

So, beyond the utility companies and phone calls, neither Meryl nor Delia had expected much contact.

Of course, they knew who this was.

Meryl glanced at Delia, who folded her lips into her mouth and raised her eyebrows. Lines formed across her forehead, and Meryl wondered just how old she was. Not much older than Meryl, probably. But a bit. Enough to show her wear and tear.

"I'll handle it," Meryl assured Delia, smoothing her shirt before striding to the front door.

She opened it with a rough tug, and it fell inside, revealing on the stoop a woman who could only be Miss Lucille Spaur of the newspaper posting.

"Lucy?" Meryl smiled and took her in. Tufts of white hair, curled matronly and classically and tucked down beneath pins gave way to a wide, kind face, lined a hundred times over what Delia had. Plastic-rimmed, oversized glasses masked the woman's eyes, but not so much that Meryl couldn't detect milky blue irises smiling back at her.

The woman clutched a leather handbag in one hand. Then, she leaned heavily upon a cane with the other, her whole frame sort of banking into it, distorting the image of the woman, a taxi cab in the street beyond, and the weedy grass of the front yard.

Meryl realized she wasn't making much of an impression yet, and she flushed a little.

"Yes," the woman replied, her voice stronger in person than it had been on the phone. "And you're Meryl?" A trembling smile overcame her wan mouth, and a breeze lifted a chunk of her wispy white hair.

"Yes, do come in. Come in," Meryl pushed the door open wider and took a step forward, naturally gripping the woman's elbow and ushering her into the house.

"Oh, my," Lucy said on a breath as she entered. "The Stevers. Oh, yes."

Meryl's smile slipped away. "You knew them?" she asked, unable to hide the accusation in her tone.

Lucy didn't notice. "I knew *of* them. I worked just down the way there." Lucy lifted a crooked finger and pointed northerly.

Now didn't seem the time to ask after Lucy's old employment. Instead, the proper thing to do would be to offer her a beverage. "Would you care for some water? Lemonade?"

"Oh, no. No, no," Lucy had made her way into the living room and was catching her breath. "I'll be just fine. I'm here on business, really."

"Aren't we all," Meryl quipped, but the joke was lost on Lucy, as she didn't know her from Adam. Or her purpose.

Then again, even Meryl didn't quite know her own purpose.

Before she had a chance to explain everything, Lucy twisted her cane into the floor and said, "Now this is the place where they found that poor woman." It wasn't a question.

Meryl and Delia exchanged a look. Delia was quick to chime in. "Yes, that's right." And then, thankfully, she changed the topic. "Lucy, hello. I'm Delia. I'm staying on here myself. As a tenant," she added with a furtive glance at Meryl.

"Delia. A lovely name. And who were your parents, dear?"

The habit of older people to inquire after one's heritage struck Meryl as charming. Warm. Something her own mother might have done.

Delia just smiled. "Oh, I'm not from here." She didn't elaborate, and Lucy had better manners than to press her. She nodded politely and looked around the living room, taking in the shape of it. The furniture. The tchotchkes that still littered the tables and corners of the place. Meryl hadn't been sure what to do with them. So, she'd dusted and oiled them and repositioned them into the same spots where she'd found them.

"So, Lucy." Meryl clapped her hands together then held one toward the sofa. "Why don't you sit, please, and I can go over the details, I suppose."

Lucy hobbled to one of the two chairs that sat across from the sofa, lowering herself shakily then taking a few breaths. "Right," she said as the other two sat at opposite ends of the sofa. "I expect you want to know what business I have seeking a housing arrangement?" Before either Meryl or Delia could reply, Lucy pushed ahead. "Well, I don't *need* an arrangement, you see. I have a perfectly lovely home on First Street. Family home. But it's got quite a staircase, you see, and I have a cat. My sweet Fiona. Fiona is her name, and, well, I had a fall last week—of course, I don't often fall, mind you. But, you see, my daughter was already on my case about improving my situation." Lucy waved her hand in the air and Meryl saw a chunky beige wrist brace.

Meryl nodded. "I can understand that. And here, it's only the stoop. You'd never have to go upstairs." She gestured to the staircase that unfurled up behind Lucy and then shook her head to herself. Here she was, speaking as though it were a done deal. As though Lucy could move in today and all three of them would ride into the sunset, nary a worry in any of their hearts. A little gaggle of geese, carving out a happiness together on the edge of Gull's Landing.

"You mentioned circumstances," Lucy pointed out. "If the circumstances happen to be the woman's death, well, I'm not unaccustomed to death. So long as I won't be sleeping in her bed, naturally." Lucy pursed her lips and twisted her handbag handles on her lap.

"Oh, right. No, no. Of course not," Meryl answered. "I meant that I'm not sure just how long I'll be keeping this place."

A quiet came in response. An uncomfortable, tense quiet. Lucy blinked behind her thick glasses. Delia sniffed.

"I had planned to flip it. Keep it over the summer and prepare it for the market by fall." Meryl shifted uncomfortably. "But I might not."

Lucy looked at Delia and twisted her handbag handles again. "I see. That's a nice idea. Might turn a profit. It's a beautiful home. Always was. But then there's the matter of its location." Her tone clipped, Lucy ran her tongue over her teeth and bit down on her lower lip, perhaps nervous at overstepping her boundaries so obviously.

"What do you mean by that?" Meryl edged forward on her seat, genuinely interested. Lucy's implication indicated there was a bigger issue at play. Something more to Mill River Road than Meryl knew about. Something that could explain the Stevers kids' abandonment of the place... or even Meryl's draw to it.

## CHAPTER 21—LUCY

Lucy apologized immediately. "It's not my place to suggest what you might or might not do with this house. And now, I must be going. My cat is surely waiting for me. Supper time, you see." Lucy wiggled her cane into position at her side. "I appreciate your meeting with me, but you're right." Lucy looked from Meryl to Delia and back again. "I'm looking for something more permanent. Something to last me beyond the summer. Something to, well, take me to the end of the line, really." She tried for laughter, but it got garbled in her throat and instead sounded like she was choking. Embarrassed, Lucy turned away from the two women and wheezed into her fist then reached for her handbag.

"Oh, please. Can't you stay a while longer?" Meryl begged. "I'd love to hear more about your thoughts on listing—or why I'd be better off *not* listing, as the case may be."

Lucy stalled, holding Meryl's gaze for a moment

longer than was natural. She might ask the same question of Meryl—couldn't *she* stay a while longer? Why the rush to unload the property, anyway? But Lucy could hear Marcia in her ear. *Be nice, Mother. Mind your business.* "I'm sure you'll fetch a pretty penny if you choose to list. As for me? I pushed myself onto you, truly, and I'm sorry for it. I'll be going."

"We called you," Delia pointed out, standing to join Meryl and Lucy. "And we gave you the address. Maybe this is worth a longer conversation, Lucy. Don't you think? You, like me, need a place to live, right?"

Lucy blinked. "I have options," she replied proudly.

"Of course, you do," Delia rushed to answer.

"My daughter, Marcia, and her husband, Chris, primarily. Beyond that, I've—" Lucy tried to stand a little taller "—I've been offered a placement with an exclusive... *community*." She narrowed her gaze on Delia as she said it, and that seemed to get the woman's attention.

"The Landing?" Delia asked, a look of alarm coloring her face.

"The Landing?" Lucy echoed back to her. "Pardon?"

"Is that where you have the housing, um, *opportunity*?" It was Meryl who inserted herself now.

Lucy frowned. "The Landing Country Club? Oh, no. I'd never live there. Too much politicking for my liking," she huffed. "No, no. It's a community for retirees, you see. Much like a country club, mind you. Just without all the drama." Even as she said it, Lucy knew this had to be a big fib. In all likelihood, there was far more drama at Golden Oaks than in the whole of Gull's Landing's hoity-toity country club.

"Oh, right. Right." Delia fiddled with her fingernails and hung her arm out loosely back toward the sofa chair as if to coax Lucy back into her seat. "What say I whip up a warm drink for each of us. And maybe a snack?"

"That'd be great, Delia. And besides, maybe Lucy knows something that I don't know. Maybe you have information that will help me make a good decision about the future of the place." Meryl smiled sadly. "Won't you, Lucy?"

Lucy considered this plea. Sure, she knew about 12 Mill River Road. She knew about the whole of the area, in truth. Maybe she wouldn't ever be living there, but would it hurt to shell out a few pearls of wisdom to a well-meaning woman such as Meryl Preston?

No.

"I'd love a bite. And a drink. Just for a little while, at least. As I said, my cat will be going mad. We have a fairly strict routine, you see."

"Routines are important," Meryl agreed, lowering back into the chair. "As a teacher, I rely on them very heavily." Delia excused herself and it was just Lucy and Meryl left to make small talk. Or big talk, as the case may be.

"You're a teacher?" Lucy sat, too, trying to sneak the breath she needed to take. She'd hate to sound huff-and-puffy. Like a little old dragon or some such thing.

Meryl nodded. "Seventh grade math. Back in Newark. That's why I have the summer to work on this old place."

"Ah. So, you have a bit of a deadline, too?"

"Somewhat. Truth be told, originally, I wanted no part

in coming here. I didn't care to see this place. I was... scared, I suppose. Of what I'd have to face."

"What, or who, convinced you to come, then?"

"The body. The woman, I mean. They needed to confirm I didn't know her. My aunt, Viola, came with me."

"And did you?" Lucy asked. "Know her?"

Meryl shook her head. "Nope. Just a... just a vagrant. They had her burial in the potter's field."

Lucy's face fell. "How sad."

"I agree." Meryl scooted deep into her chair and ran her hands down her jeans. Lucy saw their holes and noted how intentional the look was. Fashion was an odd thing. The trends. The fads.

"You know," Lucy said, "I worked for a school, too."

"You did? Did you teach?" Meryl asked, her eyes lighting up in their shared trait.

But Lucy shook her head. "No, no. I was a secretary. After my daughter started school at Gull's Landing Elementary, I took a position just down the street here, in fact."

"Down the street?" Meryl's browline furrowed. "Do you mean—"

A mischievous smile spread across Lucy's mouth. "Shearwater. Yes."

"A secretary? My, they... had it all, I suppose."

"It's a big property. All-inclusive, you might say. Sort of like Golden Oaks, I suppose."

"Golden Oaks?" Meryl asked.

Lucy nodded. "The retirement community I might go to."

"That sounds rather lovely. A retirement community. All-inclusive, too?"

"Trust me," Delia interjected, rejoining them with a galvanized tray of mugs and a platter of crackers and cheese cubes. "There's nothing lovely about Shearwater."

"I meant Golden Oaks," Meryl shot back.

Lucy looked at Delia, whose eyebrows rose knowingly. "I'm not entirely sure there's much of a difference."

"You're familiar with Golden Oaks?" Lucy accused Delia as she accepted a steaming mug of tea.

"My friend, Nancy, opened it. It's changed hands in the past year or two, though. Surely what I've heard is colored by her bias." Delia tried to smile reassuringly.

Lucy rested her tea on a wooden coaster on the table to her right. She folded her hands neatly in her lap. While she was there, she may as well make the most of it. "Let me ask you, Delia. Would you send your own mother to live at Golden Oaks?"

Delia appeared thoughtful for a moment. "That's another story. My mother would have *needed* something like Golden Oaks. Stability. A sure bet."

"Hm," Lucy murmured, picking up her mug and drawing it to her lips. "And you, Meryl? Is that your plan for your parents? A place like Golden Oaks?"

Meryl also looked a bit pensive. Lucy felt somewhat affronted that they didn't have answers on the tips of their tongues. How might Marcia reply? Was it an encouraging thing that she had a plan for Lucy? Or should Lucy be bothered by that fact? Sometimes, it was hard to know when to be bothered and when to be grateful.

"In retrospect, I'd have done anything to keep them

closer," she said at last, her eyes growing watery. "Whether that would've been Golden Oaks or my Newark condo, I'm not sure." Her brow crinkled. "I wanted them to be happy. Above all. I just—I wasn't sure they felt the same for me."

"Of course, they did," Lucy answered, laughing lightly. "All parents want is for their children to be happy."

Meryl's gaze fell to her own cup of tea. "Right. Well."

Delia and Lucy locked eyes, and the former shrugged helplessly. Maybe these two weren't as close of friends as Lucy had suspected.

It wasn't Lucy's place to make a point about mothers and fathers and their feelings over their children. But perhaps she could cast a little light on things. Assure this poor Meryl woman that certainly her parents had loved her. "You know, I think it's easy to forget that parents are human beings, too. With their own needs and wants. Insecurities, surely. I always wondered if I was right to work at Shearwater, for example. I feared I might carry some of that home to Marcia. I was caught between being an independent woman—strong and self-reliant—and being, well, a mother. I never knew which example was more important. Giving back to the community or putting my daughter above everything else."

"Surely you could have both?" Delia offered quietly.

Lucy looked at her. "Do you have children, dear?"

Delia shook her head, and Lucy realized she couldn't tell if the woman was twenty years old or forty. "No. I... No."

Lucy realized that regardless of her age, Delia was the

sort who probably *would* be a mother. Eventually, at least. Much like she became. Years later than was socially acceptable, but still. She became one just the same. "When you do become a mother, you'll see. The balance is so out of our reach when we have children. It's impossible to know when to be the example and when to be the mom. You'll see."

## CHAPTER 22—MERYL

Lucy had long since left, and it was just Delia and Meryl again. Awkwardly conjoined together in the house whose walls were beginning to shrink in on Meryl.

Before she left, Meryl and Delia had promised Lucy that if she wanted even just a temporary placement, one of the first-floor rooms was all hers. Meryl had explained, to Lucy's sympathy, that her parents had passed, and that she'd inherited the place to do with what she wanted.

Lucy had acted a tad put-off, strangely, but Meryl wasn't able to offer much more. After all, she truly didn't know if she would keep the place or not. And with Lucy's vague, ominous implication about getting 12 Mill River Road to *ever* sell, well, it was clear that Meryl would need at least the summer to make something of it.

The following Monday, they had scheduled a local gentleman to come out and help with some minor landscaping plans and a few little repairs.

But when Meryl made her way downstairs for coffee and a muffin, she found that Delia wasn't alone.

With her, on the settee in the parlor, sat an unfamiliar woman, fully decked in makeup and a chintz pantsuit.

Delia's head was in her hands, and her shoulders lifted and fell in staccato sobs. "Delia?" Meryl asked, confused.

"You must be Meryl." The flashily-dressed woman rose and reached her hand out. "Nancy Shytle. Delia's neighbor. And friend, of course."

"Good to meet you, Nancy," Meryl shook her hand then again asked, "Delia?" This time adding, "Are you all right?"

Delia peeked up miserably before dropping her head back into her hands. Nancy bent over at her waist, plucking a folded paper from the coffee table and then passing it to Meryl. "I just hate to come bearing this news, but the committee was going to mail it, and since I'm implicated herein, I knew it had to be *me* who delivered the news."

Meryl frowned and took the paper, unfolding it and reading as Nancy bit her lower lip in a grimace. "And with that, I do need to be going. I have an important meeting. Oh, Deel, honey. Please call me soon. I hate being so out of touch with you. Katherine keeps asking after you, darling. Call me." Nancy patted Delia's shoulder awkwardly then looked at Meryl, her face breaking into something resembling a smile. "Happiest wishes for your homecoming, dear."

"Homecoming?" Meryl glanced up from the page. "I'm not—I'm not from here. Just renovating."

"And hosting strangers? Don't be silly. Only true locals spend so much time in Gull's Landing." Delia winked at Meryl. "Homecoming, housewarming—anyway. If ever you're in the country club, ask for Nancy and they'll find me. I'd love to treat you to a drink and appetizers in the clubhouse. And that goes for you too, Delia," Nancy chirped. "No more moping, sweetheart!" Nancy dropped her voice and her chin and looked up at Meryl from beneath thickly coated eyelashes. "*Bryant* sure isn't moping, if you catch my drift." She winked again and raised a hand to the door. "I'll see myself out. Enjoy the day, and again, Delia!" She lifted her voice across the room, "Call me, honey. And Meryl, be careful *here*. Won't you?"

And with that, the tornado that was Nancy Shytle twisted back out of 12 Mill River Road.

"She's your *friend*?" Meryl asked, flat-voiced.

Delia looked up helplessly, shrugging her shoulders and standing, smoothing her trousers, and scrubbing her hands over her bare face.

"What is this?" Meryl gestured to the paper in her other hand. "It reads... bizarrely. Like a student council election or something."

"More like an eviction. Or a termination. I'm not sure which. I guess, both."

"Eviction from what? It doesn't reference you at all. Just Nancy Shittle."

"Shytle," Delia corrected, pronouncing the last name only slightly differently than, well, Shit-el.

Meryl just looked at her, unmoved by the whole, odd

scene. "She's running for the HOA president of The Landing? And that affects you... how?"

"*I* am the president of the HOA." Delia smirked. "They found out that I haven't been around for a little while and have taken it upon themselves to expedite the board elections."

"What? You're Julius Caesar, and Nancy is Brutus?" Meryl couldn't help but chortle until she saw Delia's face. A stricken look marred her normally smooth, genteel expression.

"I knew it was coming. I *didn't* know that my so-called country club friends would nominate my so-called *best* friend to... unseat me." A shuddering sigh fell from her lips.

Meryl gave her a soft look. "I'm sorry, Delia. That's crummy. Truly."

Delia sniffled and raised her palms. "Oh, well. Maybe I'll get back there. Who knows what could happen with the divorce? Maybe the house won't sell? Maybe Bryant will sign it over to me? I could be president again one day. Might just need to save up for a down payment."

Meryl studied her hard. "Wait a minute. You *want* to move back there? To The Landing?"

"Of course, I do," Delia shot back. "The Landing has been everything to me. I mean... forever, I've been exactly *two* things. Bryant Astor's wife. And the HOA President."

"You mean there are no term limits?" Meryl joked, but Delia just gave her a look. "Sorry," Meryl added. "How about this? You can be the president of 12 Mill River Road. Would that help?"

Delia gave her a look. "If 12 Mill River Road were a country club, then I'd take you up on that. But so far, it's a purgatory of an ancient house on a street where no one wants to live down the road from the worst place in town."

"Wow." Meryl swayed back onto her heels. "That was... quite the summary."

Delia's face turned red. "I'm sorry, Meryl. I know it's your family home. That was cold of me."

"I'm about to get a headache if I don't get my caffeine. Come on," Meryl urged Delia toward the kitchen. "Let's get breakfast. It'll do us both good. And you can explain yourself."

"Explain myself?" Delia asked nervously as they left the parlor for the kitchen, where Meryl was happy to find the coffee pot still hot and two clean mugs awaiting them, as had been their routine of late.

"The worst place in town. I assume you mean your alma mater?"

Delia gave her a weary look and they lowered into their respective seats at the table. "Shearwater, yeah. I was a ward of the state during my time there. Worst year of my life. And that's saying a lot."

Meryl had only gained glimpses into Delia's difficult childhood so far—a small memory here, a brief story there.

"It wasn't just Shearwater that was rough, either," Delia added.

"What do you mean?"

A thoughtful look overcame Delia's face. "There was a rule we had to follow. A weird rule, but looking back, it makes sense now."

"What rule?" Meryl asked, a chill prickling up her spine and into her scalp, setting her roots on fire, turning her neck hot and her heartbeat quick.

"We weren't allowed to come *here*," Delia answered casually, taking a long sip of her coffee.

"*Here*?" Meryl echoed her emphasis.

"To the abandoned house on 12 Mill River Road. *This* house. *Here*."

## CHAPTER 23—DELIA

"Why?" Meryl asked her. "Why *would* any of the Shearwater girls come here?"

"It was an abandoned *mansion*, remember. Totally interesting. Good place to meet boys or just hang out. Some girls smoked. Most, actually." Delia chuckled. "But not me," she was quick to add.

"Oh." Meryl accepted the answer and seemed to relax.

Delia smiled at her. "It wasn't haunted or anything. It was just a *haunt*, you know? The sort of place that attracts teenagers. Where they get up to no good. Anyway. That's all. Nothing for you to worry about. Just a bit of a run-down place. Not safe for kids."

"Rough," Meryl replied. "I get it. Well, hopefully by fall, it won't be rough anymore. And hopefully, it'll be sellable, too. But is that what you meant? Is that what Nancy meant? When she said to be *careful*."

Delia downed the last of her coffee. "Meryl, listen," she said, her voice as serious as she could make it. "I don't want to rain on your parade, but I have to be frank with you."

Meryl recoiled slightly.

Delia pressed on. "Mill River Road is not prized real estate. Particularly for a residential property. It doesn't hold a candle to The Landing, naturally—"

"The Landing!" Meryl cried, throwing her hands up. "How many times do I have to hear about The Landing! My God, Delia, it's not Beverly Hills over there. It's a small-town *country club*, for God's sake! This house is massive. The property around it is huge. We just need to keep at it, and it'll sell. It'll sell high, too. Just because it's not behind the gilded gates of The Landing, doesn't mean the value is lower than the best house there."

"You're wrong," Delia answered testily. "What is that expression in real estate? Location. Location. Location. And you're on Mill River Road. A hundred yards or less from Shearwater."

"You know what?" Meryl answered, finishing her coffee off and setting the mug down heavily on the tabletop. "I'm going to march over there to Shearwater and see it for myself. You make out like that place is hell on earth, then you say so is this house. Since I can see with my own two eyes that this place has all the potential in the world, then maybe you're wrong about that place, too. And besides, if you were told 12 Mill River Road is so God-awful, why were you comfortable moving in with me? You didn't hesitate, Delia. Were you *that* desperate?"

Delia's eyes watered and her throat constricted under the heat of the question and Meryl's dramatics. Delia had dealt with angry people in her life—angry strangers, even. Community members who didn't want to adhere to the "No towels hanging from your balcony" rule. Residents who were dying to paint their fences in stark blues or tasteless pinks. She'd even earned heat from Nancy. Never, however, had Delia felt so upset by a friend's harshness.

She couldn't tell if her reaction was a result of how much she'd quickly grown to care about Meryl's opinion. Or if it was because of how cruel Meryl was acting. Preferring the former to be true, Delia forced her useless tears down her throat in a hard swallow before she replied. "Yes. I suppose I *am* that desperate."

Meryl's face fell, but before she could respond to Delia, the doorbell rang.

Both jolted at the intrusion into their intimate argument.

They glanced in unison in the direction of the front door.

"The handyman," Meryl murmured. "Must be the handyman." Her face turned to Delia. "I know what that feels like, by the way," she said as she rose.

Delia squinted at her, confused. "What?"

Meryl started for the front door, but as she came to the hall, she turned, her hand on the dated green wallpaper. The wallpaper they couldn't quite decide what to do with. "Having no one. Turning to whatever or whoever will take you. I know what that feels like."

"You couldn't," Delia answered, still injured from Meryl's unkindness.

Meryl nodded. "Maybe not to your extent. But why do you think I'm here? Holed up in this... what, ancient mansion? Crumbling tudor?" She laughed quietly and turned to go. "My parents might have died recently, but they've been gone for a lot longer than that."

Delia followed Meryl to the front door, ruminating over the bizarre answer. To her, it seemed that Meryl had a nice, normal family. Quality parents who made good life choices and gave back to the world. Meryl was living proof of this, with her college degree and middleclass job security. Condo in an average American city. And, on top of it all, a massive house in the woods at the back of a popular tourist hotspot.

Although, to be fair, 12 Mill River Road wasn't going to make Meryl rich. That was true. Maybe Meryl didn't care about getting rich. But if not, why was she sitting on it? Why not just leave it behind as her own mother had? Why did it matter now?

Delia thought better of asking. After all, regardless of its location so close to the damnable home for girls, 12 Mill River Road was also *her* new home. At least, for now.

Meryl stopped short of the door, pulling aside the narrow curtain at the window to the right of it.

"What?" she said, scrunching her face when she turned back to Delia.

"What?" Delia repeated, confused.

As if to answer, Meryl tugged the door open, revealing there on the stoop a neat, polite-looking man of at least seventy-five years.

"Can I help you?" Meryl asked, pushing the screen door open as the man moved back half a step.

"Good day, miss," he answered, his snow-white mustache quivering over his lips. "Name's Charlie

Peabody, and I'm here about your handyman position. Assuming it's still available?"

Delia examined the small, old man as he introduced himself. He wore a plaid shirt tucked neatly into deep blue corduroy pants. Suspenders helped to hold the whole ensemble together. But despite the fact that he was a slight man dressed for something other than yard work, he looked the part, somehow. His neatness aside, there was a grit to him, emanating off of him. What was left of his sparse white hair was combed crossways over his head, barely disguising an ample, shining bald spot. His trimmed mustache combed pleasantly into place, and his shoes, dark work boots, scuff-free and tied just so.

"Handyman, why, yes," Meryl glanced at Delia, and they exchanged an unspoken agreement. This gentleman was far too old to be useful.

Then again, here he was on their porch, a red toolbox hanging firmly in one hand and a wooden-handled rake in the other, like something out of American Gothic. Beyond Charlie sat his boxy, olive-green Datsun, each corner sparkling in the sunlight.

Delia wanted to ask him who he was and where he'd come from. And why, why in the *world* did he want a handyman position at 12 Mill River Road?

But she needn't have asked. He answered for her without another question. "My children are all gone across the country, living their lives here and there. Wife died five years back. If I don't pick up a few odd jobs here and there, they'll throw me in a home and toss away the key, mark my words. If you'd like my references, I'll bring my address book out from the truck there and pass it your way. You'll find a clean record of hard work. That and nothing more. Save except for my kids and a long marriage. God rest her soul." He tapped the butt of the rake on the wooden porch.

Meryl and Delia looked at each other and then Meryl looked back at Charlie. "Well, then. Welcome to the country club, Mr. Peabody. You're hired."

## CHAPTER 24—LUCY

Lucy's week was up, and she found herself back to square one. With potential buyers in and out of her house at all hours of the day, the heat was on.

She refused to move in with Marcia and Chris in the end. It didn't feel right. Chris's allergies notwithstanding, it wouldn't do to become a burden to her daughter. What with her wrist still unhealed, she had no leg to stand on, proverbially, to stick around the house much longer on her own, regardless of how long it would take to sell.

So, on Tuesday, she watched as Marcia and Chris tucked her two bags—those which held the most critical of Lucy's possessions—into the trunk of Chris's bland, sand-colored sedan. Then, she tucked herself into the backseat and off they went. To Golden Oaks.

Checking into Golden Oaks was a lot like checking into a hotel, it turned out. Or a hospital, maybe. They took all the information she'd already given them with her application, this time in duplicate, triplicate, and whichever '-icate' they needed to avoid "issues."

"You'll be in Room Twelve," the attendant declared as he rounded the counter and gestured down the main hall. "Right this way."

Lucy looked at Marcia. "Now, if that isn't a coincidence," she murmured beneath her breath.

"What do you mean, Mom?" Marcia asked. They left Chris in the lobby so that Lucy could get settled.

"Room number twelve. Did you hear?"

"Is that a special number, Mom?" The way Marcia asked it, Lucy got emotional. Not at herself but at Marcia. Is this really what her daughter thought of her? That she had something of a secret rumbling deep in her heart and now was her chance to reveal it in some way... like through the number twelve. Lucy could have kicked herself. She had no such secrets. And now here she was, moving closer to her deathbed, quite literally, and without a life of secrets to speak of.

Then again, just because Lucy didn't have her *own* secrets didn't mean she wasn't privy to the secrets of others.

Mill River Road came to mind. And Shearwater. And what might have been.

The attendant explained various features of the room, which Lucy felt was wholly condescending. As though she didn't know about beds and windows and the bathroom. Pfft.

At last, there was nothing left to say. Marcia got teary, and that was Lucy's cue to whisk her back to Chris where they made urgent promises for Marcia to return very regularly.

Lucy asked one last thing of her daughter before she left Golden Oaks. "Fiona. Please, Marcia. Please phone me as soon as you have a placement for her. Please." Lucy gripped her daughter's arms roughly, and Marcia nodded.

"I promise, Mom. We'll find someone perfect. Maybe you can even visit."

Funnily enough, it wasn't her daughter she was sore over missing. It was her cat. Lucy swallowed hard, willing away a rush of tears as Marcia and Chris left, taking all of Lucy's hopes and fears with them.

She turned to find a new orderly standing behind her.

"Miss Spaur," the man said merrily, "A few others are taking sun on the back lanai. Care to join them?"

No, she really didn't, but she learned quite quickly that questions such as this one were less questions and more veiled commands. Soon enough, she was propped like a doll on a heavily cushioned seat, a paper cup of juice in her hand to match the other women's as they cracked into a round of gossip.

Now *this*, Lucy didn't mind.

She'd long missed the days of idle chatter with her own girlfriends—most dead now.

One of them, a blue-hair, wasn't very good at keeping her voice low. "He wasn't here yesterday!" she cried out, waving a knotty hand in the vague direction of the yard.

Lucy shifted in her seat to hear better.

"I swore I saw him this morning. Maybe they changed his hours," another of them replied. This one was less frantic.

"What would your husbands say, you two?" a third answered, her feathers duly ruffled.

Now Lucy was *very* curious.

"Sh. *Shh!*" the first woman crooked a finger at her lips and then pointed it indiscreetly beyond Lucy to the far side of the lawn.

Lucy turned to follow the indicator as the other women's chatter bubbled low.

It was clear the object of their giggles. A man. Not a resident, if his labor was any indication. For he was trimming a hedge, slowly. Painstakingly, in fact. He looked to be no younger than Lucy, which made her feel irritated.

She couldn't keep her trap shut any longer. "What's the big idea?" she asked the others testily.

"The big idea *indeed*." The one with uneven pink lipstick cackled.

Lucy rolled her eyes, but fortunately, the first speaker answered her question. "That there is *Charlie Peabody*. Part-time groundskeeper for Golden Oaks."

"And full-time heartbreaker," Pink Lips added, lifting a painted eyebrow.

Lucy recoiled. They were old women, for crying out loud. And he, the smallish, hedge-trimming man in a plaid shirt and suspenders, was an old man. Who were they kidding?

She shook her head.

"Go talk to him," Pink Lips said to Lucy.

"Me?" Lucy pressed her hand with the wrist brace to her sunken chest. "Why?"

"Well, I can't very well wheel myself over there with any grace," the other woman stabbed the arm of her wheelchair with a thick fingernail. Lucy wondered if orderlies did basic maintenance on these old broads or *what*.

"And say what?"

"Ask him for a light," the uptight one offered, pushing a packet of cigarettes towards Lucy.

"I don't smoke," Lucy answered. "And neither should you."

She'd overstepped her bounds on that one.

The other women bristled immediately. If they'd had pearls, they'd be clutching them, by her estimation.

It wouldn't do for Lucy to be on the outs so early in her stay. So, she pursed her lips and stood, smoothing her dress.

"Fine." She took in a breath. "I'll go."

Two of the women clapped and one cheered with a mighty, wrinkled fist. "Oh, goodie! You can introduce us!"

Lucy frowned. "You mean you've never actually met him?"

"Well, of course not. He's hired help, for goodness' sake!" Pink Lips cried.

Lifting an eyebrow of her own—not painted, mind you—Lucy just clicked her tongue and took up her cane, walking as erectly as she could toward the man.

Once she was close, she could see plain as day that he was as old as she. And, yes, there was something handsome about him. Maybe his eyes—kind and clear. Or his jawline, strong beneath the supple skin that had turned jowly.

"Hello," Lucy started, her voice firmer than she felt.

"Good day, ma'am." He lowered his trimmers and gave her a winning smile.

Lucy felt her insides liquify. Maybe those old gals were onto something.

"Can I help you with something?" he asked, his eyes twinkling.

She forced herself not to look back to the others, thinking of whatever she could to prolong their exchange. "Yes, actually," Lucy answered, growing bolder by the moment. "You see, I'm new here, and I'm not all too familiar with the rules of the road, you might say."

He chuckled sweetly then scratched the back of his head. "I could try to help. Mind you, I'm not around all that much. Just here and there for a little maintenance work. To help out the other guys." His voice, a touch craggy at the edges, was kind to match his eyes and deeper on certain words, inflecting them with soul the likes of which stirred something in Lucy she didn't realize was still there.

She swallowed. "Right, well. My question is… do you know if residents are permitted to leave the grounds as they desire?"

Her final word hung heavily between them, and a mischievous grin curled his mouth.

Lucy forced herself not to glance back at their audience.

"I, er," he started, slow to find words but quick to glance about them, as if she'd engaged him in something obscene.

Lucy flushed, but that was okay. It wouldn't hurt for a little color to plump up her cheeks during their interaction. That she could still flush at all was something of a marvel.

"Well, truth be told I'm not entirely sure, ma'am. I'd imagine so, if you had means, that is."

"Means?" Lucy asked, cocking her head ever so slightly.

He cleared his throat. "Well, sure, ma'am. If you arrange with the front desk, I'd imagine so."

Again, Lucy repeated his suggestion. "I have to arrange an outing at the front desk, then?"

"I suppose. Or at least arrange for a taxi cab. Unless you have a friend who wants to take you out."

At that, Lucy's pulse quickened. Either at the hope she might get out of Golden Oaks more regularly than she'd predicted. Or at Mr. Charlie Peabody's evident flirtation. Didn't matter which.

Although, Lucy did not have a friend who wanted to take her out.

*Yet*.

## CHAPTER 25—MERYL

Charlie was expected back on Wednesday.

Monday had gone well. Surprisingly well. After giving him a tour of the grounds, he seemed bored enough that she'd taken him to the back of the house. There, she indicated that she had little in the way of tools, to her knowledge, proving as much when she opened a rotted wooden door off the back porch to an empty space. It had likely been a shed of sorts. Or even a cellar, but it was now barren, with an inner red brick wall to match the one beneath the stairs.

Charlie had waved her off, saying he was well enough prepared with his collection of equipment. "Simple but effective," he'd declared.

And with that, he got right to it. Weeding the lawn and raking carried him into late afternoon, when the front lawn's transformation was glimmering with potential. Meryl was more than satisfied.

She wondered where this Charlie Peabody character resided. What he was doing with life and how he'd managed to keep so lively for his age, but it wasn't yet her business.

While Delia and Charlie set about their second round of weeding, Meryl took a scraper and situated herself near a particularly rough patch of the front facade. Her task was to chip off old exterior paint, sand, then prime. Eventually, a new coat would glimmer across the house, but it'd be a while. A long while. She'd need a ladder and time. Lots of time.

Time that she wasn't promised. Not if she was going back to Newark come September. Or earlier, even.

After a couple hours' work, Charlie and Delia relaxed in the kitchen with a lemonade and Meryl made a call to Viola.

There she sat, in the front hall with the black rotary, the cord tangled about her fingers as she waited for her aunt to answer.

When she did, Meryl rushed to form a greeting. "Viola, hi. It's Meryl. Listen, I'm smack dab in the middle of some great repairs on this place. I think we really have a chance to restore it and make a profit."

"Meryl, slow down," Viola chided.

She didn't. "But I need more funds if I'm going to finish in my time frame."

"Time frame?" Viola asked. "What is your time frame, then?"

"I gotta get back to Newark by late August, at the outside."

"And, what?" Viola cried over the line. "You wanna sell the house by then?"

"That's the idea, Viola." Exasperation crept into

Meryl's tone. "Anyway, I'm not sure I can finish alone. I mean... I have a little help. A friend is here with me. And we hired a groundsman to work on the yard, too. But this place needs more. Paint—inside and out. A few new appliances. I don't think I can foot it without a little seed money. Have you spoken to the estate attorney? How are the other property sales going?" Meryl asked, in reference to her parents' other rentals and their Newark home.

She was met with a pause.

Another moment later, Meryl asked, "Aunt Viola? Are you there?"

"I'm here, honey. I'm here. Listen, Meryl, I have spoken with the lawyers. And the banks."

"The banks?" Meryl frowned. She knew Viola was named as a co-executor. She had full access to all the information. This was a good thing, since Meryl's interest was so completely diluted. At least... until now. But the banks?

"There's no money, Meryl," Viola whispered flatly.

"Yet?" Meryl prompted, certain an explanation was coming.

"There isn't now, and there won't be. Meryl, I figured you had some inkling—"

"Inkling of what?" Meryl twisted away from the kitchen, shrouding herself in as private a way as she could.

"They were in debt up to their gills, Meryl."

Meryl shook her head. "That can't be. They were about to buy a new property."

"Trade. It was a trade deal. To cover the mortgage on another, they had plans to make an arrangement with a slumlord up north. It was a scam anyway, though. He'd never have settled for anything fair. They'd have dug themselves deeper."

Meryl continued shaking her head, slowly. "Viola, no. How could they go to Rome? The pilgrimage? Surely they couldn't afford that if they were in debt."

"I offered to pay for the flight. Their lodging and food would have been covered by the Children of Fatima Foundation." Viola hesitated. "Meryl, this is what they did. How are you—how didn't you know?" It was now Viola who sounded utterly surprised. "Meryl, they were practically destitute."

Dumbfounded, Meryl opened her mouth to respond. Nothing came out.

"Meryl, honey? Are you there?"

She groped for the right words. At last, something came. "And 12 Mill River Road? Is it, what? Collateral? Will it cover the others?"

"Oh, no," Viola answered. "Your parents were cleverer than that, fortunately. The deed for 12 Mill River Road has been in your name for years, Meryl."

"How come you didn't tell me?" Meryl accused.

"I didn't know that part," Viola replied. "I knew they were in hot water, and I was surprised to know they kept the Mill River house... but then, it made sense, too."

A voice came from the kitchen. "Everything okay?" It was Delia, naturally.

Meryl glanced at her and nodded urgently then dipped her chin back to the receiver. "Viola, I need to get off the line soon. But... is there anything I can do?"

"No, honey. I am sorting through things with the banks and the lawyers. I'll call you if I need you."

"All right then. I'm—Viola, I'm sorry."

"Don't apologize. This was never your fault, Meryl," Viola's voice turned sharp. An aunt's warning against guilt. "You take that house and do with it what you will. Restore it, sure. Sell it, definitely. Then, take the money and run, Meryl. You don't need that old place weighing you down. No sir."

At that, they ended the call, and Meryl returned to the kitchen, Delia still at the table. Charlie nowhere to be seen.

"Where's Charlie?" she asked Delia.

"Back to work. I can hardly keep up with him. Boy, do I hope to be that fit when I'm his age." Delia's face fell. "Meryl? What's wrong? What is it?"

Meryl slid into the empty chair next to her, reaching for her own untouched glass and sliding it her way before taking a long, thoughtful drink. If drinks could be thoughtful. Everything turned thoughtful. Every move of her hand, every breath. It was full of thoughts. Of what Meryl was to do next.

She looked at Delia. "Bad news, I suppose."

Delia waited, her face impassive, if a touch concerned.

"I won't be getting any windfall from my parents' death." She cringed upon saying it. It came out all wrong. Tears threatened to wash out of her eyes. She forced them down with another gulp of lemonade. "That's not what I meant," she managed, her gaze settling on the kitchen window, a view to where Charlie had started weeding the backyard.

"Were you... expecting something in particular?" Delia asked then quickly took back her question. "I'm sorry. Not my business."

"It is, probably," Meryl replied. "It is your business. You're here helping me. You're practically my partner in all of this. And I'm sorry about that."

"You don't have to be sorry, Meryl," Delia answered. "Your heart is broken. Why apologize for that?"

"Because we can't finish this project," Meryl answered softly. "There will be no hiring painters. No new appliances. We'll continue to line dry the clothes on that droopy old thing." She pointed through the window above the sink where they could spy the sagging line, filled from post to post with their clothes.

"I don't mind that. And we can do the painting."

"I don't see how we can finish in a summer's time," Meryl said lamely. "If it's on our shoulders, and if we have no spare money, this place will return to square one. I never should have come here. It was a waste. Useless." She flicked a glance at Delia. "I'm sorry I got you into this."

"Sorry?" Delia's face twisted. "You saved me, Meryl. If it weren't for you and this house, I'd be stuck in some tenement in Wildwood. Or worse. There are no rentals in Gull's Landing. None in my price range. You *saved* me."

Meryl closed her eyes, knowing full well that Delia was acting dramatically. Knowing full well how much she'd come to love their oddball situation and budding friendship. How curious she was about the history of 12

Mill River Road and the bizarre little boardinghouse down the street. How much she was coming to enjoy Gull's Landing. They'd planned to go to the beach for the first time that afternoon. Dinner on the boardwalk. It was... idyllic, actually. Mounds better than Newark and her sanitized condo with its HOA fees and two flights of stairs and—

"Delia," she said. Too loud. Abruptly. Delia startled. "Delia," Meryl repeated. "What if we stay?"

## CHAPTER 26—DELIA

Delia didn't have an answer. Well, she *did*. And it was *yes!* A million times *yes!*

But that was entirely self-serving and short-sighted. Who knew? In a month's time, she might have already been swept off by a handsome stranger. Or Bryant would return and beg her forgiveness, and she'd sashay and sally until she convinced him to give her the house back under the false pretense that she'd reunite with him, only to then thwart his advances and live happily ever after on Albatross Avenue as Queen of the HOA for ever and ever. Amen.

Hey. A girl could dream, right?

Charlie remained in the backyard, puttering away productively. More productively than either Delia or Meryl felt like being at that very moment. The heat of the day coupled with the promise of an early evening on the boardwalk, sang to Delia. She could use the girl-time. And was now the appropriate time to undermine her growing friendship?

Or were friends supposed to be brutally honest?

Delia opted for a happy medium. "I think your best option, Meryl, *truthfully*, is to keep this place. If you can. Maybe that means you work on it slowly, over time. You don't rush it. Maybe that means you stay in Gull's Landing if you want. But what about your condo? Your teaching position in Newark?"

There. Delia struck the right notes. Hit the right points. She managed to uphold the integrity of their friendship while gently pointing out to Meryl that selling was a bad idea, but that who knew what the future held? Maybe Meryl was meant to keep the place... even if Delia didn't stick around.

And yet, Meryl's response proved that Delia had still, effectively, slapped her in the face. "You don't think I could sell."

Delia shook her head. "That's not what I said at all. I said I think you'd be crazy *to* sell. If it were me, I'd keep it. No question." Delia lifted both arms. "Look around you, Meryl. You *own* a mansion. Free and clear, right?"

Meryl nodded half-miserably.

"And you want to unload it... why? To bank cash?"

Meryl seemed to consider the question, her face pinched and thoughtful. "To move on," she said at last, half-heartedly.

Delia wasn't sure how to respond. All that came out of her mouth was, "Oh."

But that was enough, apparently. Enough to screw Meryl's courage in. "I can't do it, Delia. I can't sell. I mean seriously. I won't be able to. Not in this condition. And I don't know that I want to."

"And Newark?" Delia asked quietly, bracing for her friend to find herself conflicted all over again.

But Meryl wasn't. She wasn't very conflicted. If anything, she seemed... hopeful. "Maybe that's what I'll do," she said, her voice lifting in revelation. "Maybe I'll sell the *condo*. And... stay here."

Delia tempered her own growing excitement over the thought. If Meryl stayed, then she could stay in Gull's Landing forever. She would have someone. Someone other than icy Nancy and the HOA board. Someone other than Bryant, naturally—of course, she didn't have him anymore, anyway.

All of a sudden, Delia's own future stretched before her. Long and happy and fulfilling. "You could apply at Shearwater!" she cried, her joy getting the better of her.

"Apply at Shearwater?" Meryl frowned now. "But it's not a school."

"It has a school. It has teachers and everything. It's huge, Meryl. Seriously. Take it from me. They could use someone like you, I'm sure."

Meryl studied her hard, as if to discern whether Delia was being honest and sincere. As if to discern all of the future right there, in Delia's stare. It was a lot of pressure to carry: a new friend's fate, that was.

"I'm sure they aren't hiring," Meryl reasoned at last.

Delia shrugged. "We could walk down there and see. You never know. A place like that has high turnover, I'd imagine."

And just like that, it was settled.

They told Charlie they were off for an errand, entrusting him not only with his own tasks but also with access to the house. Delia wasn't entirely certain about how valuable the furniture and decor and various trinkets of the house really were. They were antique in *nature*, but their quality was questionable at best. After all, when Delia had first moved in, Meryl had told her about finding graffiti in a back bedroom and trash in the deepest corners of the house. Cigarette butts, soda bottles. The like.

Those things left behind by vagrants and wayward teenage girls, alike. The remnants of a transient life full of challenges and things perhaps more important than worrying over whether you were trespassing or littering. Things as important as survival.

## CHAPTER 27—MERYL

She was crazy. Out of her mind. Unreasonable and wild as a hog in heat.

But Meryl had nothing to lose. Except a piece of her mother's history. And that might be the costliest thing she *could* lose.

The Shearwater School for Girls declared itself frankly with a wooden sign that bore its title. And beneath the name of the place, an added description so that passersby knew to steer clear: Boarding School and Group Home.

Meryl immediately felt a softness form for the girls who roamed within. She glanced at Delia, sizing her anew, as a former resident. How Delia had made such a life for herself, well, it was no wonder she didn't want an apartment or a shelter or a charity. She wanted something better than that. And if 12 Mill River Road was better than her other options, Meryl's sympathy grew exponentially.

"It looks exactly the same," Delia murmured as they

walked down the dirt drive, stopping again at an outer iron gate, several feet higher than Meryl and Delia stood tall. Black. Imposing and fearful.

"Is it a boarding school or a prison?" Meryl cracked, but Delia didn't laugh. "How do we... get in?" she added, searching the perimeter for any form of entry.

"There," Delia pointed. Yards to the left was, in fact, a gate. It blended well with the rest of the fence, camouflaged in its blackness. A small doorbell, of sorts, was hidden between two pickets.

Meryl pressed it and stepped back. Delia fell in next to her, and together they stared at the place.

In many ways, it resembled 12 Mill River Road. Same architecture. Same size—if not a bit bigger. The yard between where they stood and the front door was properly maintained, however. In fact, looking at Shearwater, Meryl imagined what her own house *could* be. And it was then she realized that was how she *saw* 12 Mill River Road. As her own house.

The front door opened, and out stepped a woman clad in a cornflower blue shift dress. Of an indefinite age and disposition, she walked down a bland cement path and to Meryl and Delia, offering just a small smile as she neared them.

"Hello," the woman said. "Do you have an appointment?"

Meryl and Delia exchanged a look, and then Meryl answered, "No, I'm afraid not. We're—well, we're your neighbors," she added, pointing back toward the street and down. "I'm Meryl Preston."

"Preston?" The woman's smile fell into a deep frown.

Meryl nodded. "That's right. I've just inherited the Stevers property down the way there. You might know it?"

A pause, and then, "Of course," the woman said. "Is that why you're here?"

Confused, Meryl shook her head. "I mean, well. I'm here to introduce myself, I suppose. And to inquire about any open positions."

"Open positions?" It was becoming a game of echoes. First Meryl, then this frowning woman.

Delia cleared her throat. "Are you the headmistress?" she asked. It was clear Delia spoke the language of Shearwater, and Meryl was silently grateful she'd come along.

"No." At last, the woman answered rather than copied. "We don't have a headmistress. We have a *headmaster*." She bristled. "I'm Margot, the administrative assistant."

Meryl knew this term was a fancy way of saying secretary. Margot was anything but fancy, clearly. But she was also anything but a secretary, it seemed.

"Is the *headmaster* available?" Meryl asked, mirroring the woman's tone.

She huffed and sighed and huffed again, then finally withdrew a heavy-looking brass key from her dress pocket and unlocked and opened the gate. "Come in, won't you?" she offered through her teeth. "I'll have you wait in the foyer while I see about it."

They followed her up through trimmed, green grass along the bland walkway and in through a dark wooden door.

Once inside, Margot ushered Meryl and Delia into

two metal-framed chairs by the door. Across from them, a sterile-looking desk with a stack of textbooks, strangely. A lamp with a green shade glowed nearby, although sunlight lit the room through the windows.

After she disappeared into a nearby room—what must have been a parlor when and if the building was once a home—Meryl whispered to Delia. "She recognized my last name, I think."

Delia just shrugged. "Maybe your parents donated to Shearwater?"

Meryl considered this. It was a good thought. Perceptive of Delia and very likely true. After all, the Prestons had put charity above all else.

Even Meryl.

"Miss Preston?"

The voice shook Meryl from her reverie. She lifted her head toward the parlor to see a surprisingly... *attractive* man standing there. Margot was nowhere to be seen.

Meryl forgot herself for a moment, until Delia nudged her.

"Oh." She stood, unsteadily. "Yes, hello. *Headmaster*," she added awkwardly.

To his credit, the man broke into a chuckle. "John Quinn. Good to meet you."

"Meryl," she said, pressing a hand to her chest. She then gestured to Delia. "This is my friend, Delia." Swallowing, Meryl couldn't help but assess him. He came across as every bit the headmaster and nothing of a boarding school administrator. "You run Shearwater?" she asked, her gaze falling from his thick, dark hair to his sharp jawline. Silver-framed, round spectacles and brown leather patches at his elbows said professor, but his height coupled with the chiseled bone structure said college football coach. Not that Meryl knew about college football coaches, but the man who stood before her, as the leader of a girls' school, seemed at once everything the part and nothing the part.

She couldn't help but rake her hair in a loose gesture over her head and suck her cheeks in.

"Yes and no," he answered her, his voice gentle but firm. "I run the school and oversee the day-to-day operations for the boarding students. It's the case managers, faculty, and staff, however, who do the real work here."

"Sounds like a full house of employees," Meryl replied. "You may have even answered my question."

Mr. Quinn stepped all the way out of his door frame and to the side before gesturing back inside. "Won't you come in? Have a seat, and we can discuss—" his eyes narrowed on Meryl, but his brows twitched in uncertainty "—whatever it is you'd like to discuss?"

Meryl and Delia accepted his invitation by way of synchronous nods before striding into the room. Meryl braced herself to find the cool Margot within, waiting with a scowl, but the room was empty save for dark wooden furniture. An open doorway at the far corner explained Margot's disappearance.

"My secretary, Margot," Mr. Quinn began as all three of them lowered into seats. Meryl and Delia in a pair on the far side of his desk. Mr. Quinn inside of the broad wooden thing. "The woman who greeted you?"

Meryl nodded. "Yes. It was generous of her to let us in,

I suppose. I know we didn't have previous arrangements, so thank you for seeing us on the spot."

"Oh, it's nothing," he waved them off. "The girls are in classes. I'm doing paperwork, and so I welcome the break. What I was going to say, though, was that Margot knows you? Knows your name?"

Meryl glanced at Delia, who glanced back, her eyes answerless.

"Me?" Meryl replied.

"Whichever of you is Miss Preston." He chuckled again, leaning back in his seat, entirely comfortable, it would appear, that he held the conversation by its roots, shaking Meryl and Delia free of their moorings.

"I'm Meryl Preston," Meryl acknowledged. "You had it right. Sorry, I just—I don't know her—Margot, I mean. I'm not sure how she'd know me. Maybe it's my mother? Gladys Preston? Or my father?"

Mr. Quinn's smile slipped away, and his jaw tensed visibly. "Gladys Preston." He said like an afterthought.

"I suppose she wasn't a popular property owner by the end," Meryl attempted. "I know she let it get bad. I'm sorry. I hope the state of my mother's house hasn't... affected Shearwater or any other locals." This was a lukewarm apology. A half-apology, really. Meryl did not believe the house could have impacted Shearwater. Rather, it was more likely that Shearwater's presence would have impacted 12 Mill River Road.

Mr. Quinn was partially moved, judging by a softening of that jawline. After a quiet moment, he worked up a reply. "It's quite alright."

Meryl frowned. *What* was quite alright? She didn't do anything. She had nothing to apologize for.

"Mr. Quinn," she went on, losing interest in inquiring about a job. "I am a certified math teacher. I currently teach in Newark—seventh grade pre-Algebra. But I'm qualified to teach grades six through twelve and any level of mathematics within that grade range. I came by because, well, I might stay on here. In Gull's Landing. Delia here mentioned that there could be an opening, or that we might ask, at the very least. That's why we're here, you see."

His face lit up, and he shook his head, as if to expel the contents of their penultimate topic. "Well, then," he leaned forward, lacing his hands across the top of his desk. "Now that's quite the curveball. I take it you saw our listing?"

"Listing?" Meryl's eyes again flashed to Delia, who smirked knowingly. She smiled at her friend. "Why, no. I didn't realize there was one. I figured we were coming over on a hunch. A neighborly one, I suppose. Is it a secondary math opening, by chance? Do you even hire subject experts? I suppose I'm not entirely certain of the educational structure in place in an institution such as this."

He passed his hand through the air as if cutting away the nonsense. "To be perfectly frank, we're flexible. Not all of our wards actually attend classes here. We have twenty-five, at present. Only ten remain here for their school days. The remainder attend the local public school, and I'd be imprudent not to mention that the local public school would hire you in a heartbeat, Miss Preston."

"Meryl," she emphasized, locking eyes with him. She felt heat in their shared look. As if a pulse of electricity throbbed through the air, joining them in the ether. It was ridiculous, and *clearly*, Meryl needed to get out more.

"Meryl," he murmured, clearing his throat. "Anyway, we have the funding to keep two tutors on staff. They function almost like private tutors for those girls here who are most incapable of attending public school. One usually covers humanities. The other, math and science. Coincidentally, that one is our current opening. Miss Havisham had to take her leave in May. She won't return. However, it's not a secondary-exclusive position. You'd be working with our wards ages five through eighteen."

"Five through eighteen. That's quite a gap. And you have ten who stay for their lessons? May I ask their ages?" Excitement grew in her chest as though a dozen butterflies had hatched from their cocoons. She'd worked at her current site for going on twenty years. To make a change would be… frightening at worst. Exhilarating at best.

"Presently, all ten are over the age of nine."

"Nine years old. That would be, what? Fourth grade or so?"

"That's right. I believe the youngest takes fourth grade lessons."

"And the reason they take their lessons privately?"

Mr. Quinn tugged at the collar of his shirt and dipped his chin, lowering his voice. "It's a matter of confidentiality." He glanced briefly at Delia. "Rest assured that if you apply in earnest, and if we hire you—" a grin flickered on his lips, bemused, apparently, by his own hypothetical "—we'd disclose any relevant information. No doubt you'd fill in the holes when you work with the young ladies."

Something in Meryl told her to strike while the iron was hot. That this was it. This was one of those moments in life where you said yes. Because if she said no, she feared very seriously that she'd wind up in the exact same position she'd found herself just weeks earlier: living with the sort of regret that would never, *ever* go away.

"I'd like to interview," she said with a finality that left no chance for Mr. Quinn or Delia to talk her out of it.

## CHAPTER 28—LUCY

On Thursday, Lucy had a visitor. This was nice, because the groundskeeper called Charlie Peabody hadn't appeared at Golden Oaks yet. He was probably out galavanting with any number of local spinsters. Lucy didn't care about him or anything.

She mainly just cared about Fiona.

"Mom, how is it going?" Marcia's words were slick with guilt as they sat across from each other on Golden Oaks' lanai, the most tolerable locale in all of the institution.

Granted, even Lucy couldn't deny a certain appeal about the place. For those in equal or worse condition to Lucy, it could be argued that Golden Oaks had quite a lot to offer. Social events. Good food. Cleanliness. It occurred to Lucy that if she had ever wanted to hole up in an old folks' home, well, she was in the right one. One she might grow used to with time. Again, if it wasn't for the matter of Fiona.

Lucy's hand propped like a scarecrow's around a mug

of coffee. Marcia held hers to her mouth, the styrofoam dwarfed in her daughter's long, smooth fingers. It was a shame, truly, that Marcia was there. A shame for Marcia, that was. She was young with a world of her own. That she felt it such a duty to "swing by" on her way to the boardwalk about killed Lucy.

Wouldn't everything have been better if she'd stayed in her own house, staircase or no staircase? She could have slept in the living room. Really, she could have.

"I'm fine, but how is Fiona? Have you heard about her yet?"

"I was wondering if you'd like to come with me today, Mom?" Marcia asked.

Lucy frowned. "Did you hear me? Fiona. How's Fiona? Tell me about who she's with. Where do they live? Can I visit?"

Marcia's eyes clouded over. "I figured you'd like to get out, and since you're free to go whenever—so long as you have a ride—well, why not? It's a gorgeous day. Chris is working late tonight. We can get cocktails at Maeve's after."

Anger rose up in Lucy's chest. She paused just before blowing her gasket, her eyes flashing as if there might be an orderly around who'd kick this woman out. Daughter or no daughter. She kept her cool. "Is she at your house?"

"Now, Mom, I don't want you to get upset," Marcia said slowly, carefully. As if—as the kids would say. As if one didn't become upset when warned not to get upset!

"You killed her, didn't you," Lucy's voice rumbled low, quaking with the accusation.

Marcia pushed air between tight lips. "*Mom*, be serious! I did *not* kill Fiona." She laughed, glancing nervously around. She was lying. Had to be. But then came a worse admission. "She's at the Farm."

Lucy's mouth fell open and a sob worked up into her throat. She clamped her hand over it to avoid a scene, recovering only enough to gasp, "The animal shelter? You left her at the *animal shelter*?" The Animal Farm, usually reduced to just the *Farm*, was Gull's Landing's answer to the problem of unwanted or unowned dogs and cats.

"Well, gee, Ma, would you have preferred I'd poisoned her? It's a safe place for cats and dogs! Safe as anyone's house. Safer, even!"

Lucy boiled and boiled at her daughter's lack of decency. "Is this who I raised?" she asked, her mouth a knot of fury.

"A decent person who knows that a human being's health outweighs that of a housecat? Yes, actually. That's exactly who you raised."

"I'm not talking about Chris's so-called allergies. I'm talking about *you*. Too lazy to do the groundwork and find a good home for the most important thing in my life." Lucy didn't care about her implication that Marcia came in second to Fiona. She was seething. Seething! And here was Marcia, making excuses for unloading Fiona at an animal shelter like yesterday's trash.

Just as Marcia opened her mouth, probably to high-pressure Lucy into sitting in a splintery Adirondack chair on the beach and getting sand in all her wrinkles... Just as Marcia opened her mouth to distract Lucy from the painful truth that she'd been *tricked*, an orderly appeared.

"Miss Spaur?"

Lucy glanced at the woman, confused and blinking. "What?" she spat, then steadied herself. "Yes?" she added, her voice as soft as she could make it under the circumstances. She needed to get out of Golden Oaks. She needed to go to Fiona and free her of that awful place and find a real home for her. A good one.

"The bus is here if you'd like to take a trip to the nursery with a few others."

"The nursery?" Lucy scrunched her face.

"Yes, it's a place where you can buy plants for your gard—"

"I *know* what a nursery is," Lucy answered, flicking a huffing glance at Marcia. An idea occurred to her.

This could be it. This could be her chance. She could finagle a way over to the Farm. Maybe smuggle Fiona into Golden Oaks... or... or *something*.

"Oh, yes," Lucy went on, a coy smile curling across her lips at last. "I had planned to join that, um, that *expedition*." She grabbed her cane. The orderly took the cue to help her stand. "I can't make the beach today, dear," she sneered to her daughter. "I've got other plans, you see."

And with that, she shuffled onto the handicap bus and off the grounds of Golden Oaks.

What Lucy did not realize, though, was that she wasn't returning.

## CHAPTER 29—MERYL

John Quinn called first thing on Thursday morning. Meryl hadn't been expecting his phone call, but with so few inbound calls at 12 Mill River Road, she was unsurprised to hear his voice on the line.

And, to tell the truth, she was a little exhilarated. "Yes, this is she," Meryl replied when his husky voice requested to speak with Miss Meryl Preston.

"Miss Preston," he went on, "I spoke with the other tutor we have on staff along with my secretary, and we'd be honored to offer you the position of science and math tutor here at Shearwater—if you're still interested, that is?"

She took a moment to collect her thoughts, twisting the phone cord in her hand briefly before answering. "Won't you give me a day to ensure my affairs are in order, Mr. Quinn?"

"Absolutely," he answered warmly. "And please, call me John."

"And call *me* Meryl," she answered. "Should I ring you back or—?"

"You can call or swing by. I'll be here all day. All night, too." He chuckled then quickly added, "I mean... I only mean to say that I live here."

This surprised Meryl, in fact. "You do? With the girls?" It came out all wrong. She covered her face in her free hand and started to backpedal, but he laughed good-naturedly.

"I have a back house. The girls call it the Shearwater Shack."

Meryl shared his chuckle and let out a breath. John Quinn was nothing like she'd have imagined a headmaster of the formidable boardinghouse. He wasn't smarmy or grimy, and neither was the building, itself. Whatever Delia's experience, things had clearly changed there. Surely the property value at 12 Mill River Road would not be tugged down by Shearwater.

Then again, was Shearwater's reputation perhaps tugged down by 12 Mill River Road?

Meryl made a silent personal pact to find out. Maybe that was the missing piece to all of this. That's what she'd been searching for in her mother's abandoned ancestral home: something dark and sinister that had thrown shock waves across the seaside town. Some icky secret that hobos and vagrants didn't mind.

But that locals maybe did.

After ending the phone call with John, Meryl replaced the phone gently in its cradle, her pulse quick and breaths shallow. In the span of a day, her world had been flipped upside down. She'd have to contact Newark, figure out the dynamics of selling her condo—would she even sell it? Hell, maybe it would make more sense to rent the place out. Her parents would have liked that.

"Well?" Delia appeared at the doorway to the kitchen. "How'd it go?"

"I got the job," Meryl answered in a whisper. She raised her voice and repeated herself. "I got the job?" It came out like a question the second time, but her face split into a smile.

Delia strode to her and grabbed her arms. "Are you happy?" she asked, gripping Meryl with a force.

In her life, Meryl couldn't quite remember a time when anyone had ever asked her that. More often, it had been, *Are you well?* Or *Does this work for you?* Once, in a relationship that had dragged on years past its expiration date, somebody did happen to ask, *Are you unhappy?* Meryl knew the answer to that without a doubt.

And now, she realized, she knew the answer to her new friend's question. She squeezed Delia back and said, "Yes. Despite it all, *yes*. I am happy."

Delia's grip tightened and she bounced up and down on the balls of her feet in a little celebratory dance. "I'm happy for you then," Delia gushed.

Meryl's smile slipped away. "Delia," she said, suddenly all too aware of everything that had transpired in the past two weeks—and the speed at which it had all transpired. From turning her mother down, to learning of her parents' death... to joining Viola in Gull's Landing to prove she didn't know the poor dead vagrant, to whipping

12 Mill River Road into shape and deciding *to hell with it! I'll stay! I'll work and live here and figure out why I'm so utterly drawn to this bizarre little place!* "What about you?" she asked at last, looking hard at the pretty red-headed orphan of a woman. A woman betrayed more earnestly than Meryl had ever been. Ever would be, even.

Delia's eyes closed momentarily before she looked back at Meryl. "I could be," she said.

"What would make you happy?" Meryl asked, fearing a bad answer. Fearing that Delia would say she'd be happy if Bryant returned to her. If she could find a good rental in The Landing... or even, make a purchase there. If her old life came calling again. It wasn't Meryl's business to decide what was good or bad for Delia. But that's what happened when you lived and worked with someone and came to know them quickly and intimately. You knew what was good for them. Or bad. You knew it clearly.

"Delia," Meryl said, before she could respond, "If I'm staying here, at least for the next school year, then you should, too. Right?" she added, as if seeking permission for them to carry on in this odd little arrangement.

Delia smiled. "I'd like that. I'd like that quite a lot, Meryl. But I have to do something else."

"What?"

"I have to get a job. I can't just... I can't just be a hanger-on. That's not me, Meryl."

"I'll hire you, then."

"Hire me for what?" Delia laughed lightly. "You'll be making little at Shearwater, I'd imagine. And what work do you have for someone like me?"

"Someone like you with a history of cleaning toilets and pulling weeds?" Meryl tapped her index finger against her lip, her eyes searching the hall expressively. "Gee, I wonder." A wry smile shaped her mouth, and Delia rolled her eyes in response. "Seriously, Delia. There's so much to do here. And it's a huge house. If I'm teaching full-time come fall, then how will I get anything done?"

"You'll have Charlie Peabody, no doubt," Delia pointed out. "He seems to be over the moon to work here. Speaking of Charlie," Delia frowned, "where is he? Wasn't he supposed to come by this morning?"

"I sent him to The Greenery with a little list," Meryl answered. Just before I spoke with John. He'll be back before lunch, and then we can start working. But until then, let's make a list."

"A list?" Delia asked.

"Yes. I like lists. And if you and I are staying here, and if I'm hiring you to keep the place up and tend the gardens alongside ol' Charlie, then we need to make a list. After all, we won't just live here as a pair of spinsters, will we?"

"Well, I'm not sure what you mean," Delia confessed. "I figure we take a year to make a plan, right? Maybe by then, my luck will have changed. Maybe you'll miss Newark. Who knows?

Meryl nodded. "Right. Or maybe we'll both fall in love with this place. Maybe we'll find a side project. Something bigger than a teaching gig down the road or a part-time job housekeeping. Maybe we'll hatch a dream or two here, you know?"

"So, you mean to make a list of our dreams?" Delia asked, clearly amused and somewhat cynical.

But Meryl was determined. "Exactly. A list of all the things this place could be. All the things we might become here."

## CHAPTER 30—LUCY

Lucy remembered when The Greenery had first opened its doors. It wasn't too long back—when Bohemian was in fashion—and all of a sudden spider ivy and fluffy ferns had adorned every windowsill in Gull's Landing. She, herself, had never much been one for fads, but then... she wasn't taking the Golden Oaks bus into town to buy a potted plant.

Oh, no.

She was taking the bus to The Greenery because it just so happened to be closer to the Farm than Golden Oaks, which sat at the very corner of town, far out of the way and hidden from the public's consciousness.

Of course, Lucy wasn't entirely certain what she'd do once she made her way there—either to the nursery or to the animal shelter. She figured she'd let fate intervene, insomuch as it would.

Perhaps she'd slip away for an hour, reclaim Fiona handily, tuck the cat into her knitting bag, then return to her group and keep Fiona in her private bath. It wasn't a great idea. But it was a start.

They unloaded in painful slowness, one by one, easing out of the bus and onto the front walk of the nursery in a huddle until the leader, a cranky orderly, told everyone they had exactly half an hour. Then it was back on the bus for lunch on First Street.

Lucy had no interest in luncheoning on First Street, and had she known they'd be taking a detour, she'd have opted out, happy to find another way. How could she hide Fiona for an hour or two at a cafe? She couldn't. Plain and simple.

"Pardon me," she said to the orderly. "Is there a way I can just, well, do my shopping then return to Golden Oaks?"

The orderly looked her up and down. "You tell me, darlin'."

Lucy hated it when younger people used familiarisms with her. Pet names as though she'd made the full circle back to childhood. Not yet, she hadn't.

"I'll take that as a yes, then? I can ask the driver to drop me at Golden Oaks?"

The orderly shook her head. "We're on a schedule. If you want to make a detour for your pills or something, you'll have to call for a private car or a cab." She raised her eyebrows as if to suggest Lucy was anything but capable of doing either.

"I'll just do that, then," Lucy snapped back, narrowing her gaze on the awful woman.

The others, including the orderly, left and went into the structure. Lucy remained there briefly, eyeing the street in both directions, anchoring herself along the geographic grid in order to make her escape.

If she was acquainted well enough, then she knew the Farm was east of The Greenery. She'd need to head that way, along a stretching sidewalk for probably a mile. Maybe more.

Lucy could *not* walk a whole mile. She could hardly sit in the bus for a mile. There had to be another option. She glanced back to the bus, about to ask the driver to break the rules and the schedule and sweep her away on a highly secretive, highly sensitive mission.

But she was cut off. "Say!" a man's voice startled her from behind. Lucy turned to see none other than Charlie Peabody standing behind her, a rusted wagon at his side. In it burst green plants and flowers. "Don't I know you?"

Lucy flushed and staved off a grin. "Loosely," she answered, keeping her expression and tone as casual as possible. Anyway, she didn't have time for chit-chat. She needed to hijack the bus, get to the Farm, grab Fiona, and get back to The Greenery before Nurse Ratched ever knew she was gone.

"Miss Lucy from G.O."

"G.O.?" Lucy's eyes danced from him to the bus and back again. "Sorry?"

"Golden Oaks. That's what I call it. Go to G.O. We all go there, eventually. Or the lucky ones do, I s'pose." He laughed at his joke, if that's what it was meant to be, and Lucy took the opportunity to excuse herself.

"Right, well. I have to, er, run an errand before the group returns, you see. So, I'd better be off."

"An errand?" Charlie asked, "They let you charter that

thing for a side excursion, eh? See, now *that's* why people love Golden Oaks. The freedom!"

She smirked. "Well, we'll see just how far I get. I'm not entirely sure the driver *will* take me, truth be told."

He eyed her. "I'll give you a ride, if you'd like."

Lucy's neck grew hot. Her hand wobbled on her cane and she was suddenly aware of the lipstick she'd applied that morning. Aware of her blouse—the floral pattern pretty and feminine and worn for Marcia's visit, specifically. For the hope of news about Fiona. Good news. News that hadn't come.

Charlie Peabody was a stranger to her, really. Dangerous? Probably not. Still, she didn't know him. And what if he told the orderly? What if he derailed everything?

"Where did you need to go?" he asked.

She swallowed, then glanced down the road as if her destination would suddenly appear in the middle of the street only yards off. It did not. "The Farm. I need to—I need to see about an animal there. A cat."

"Your cat?" he asked, his voice low, his gaze growing shifty. She could sense he was uncomfortable now. Though about her generally or the fact that she was a bit of a troublemaker... she wasn't sure which.

She rolled her shoulders back best she could. "Why, yes. My daughter mistakenly left my cat at the Farm. I'm going to collect her."

Charlie scratched the back of his neck and adjusted the wagon handle in his other hand. "And take her to G.O.?"

Lucy fixed him with a desperate look. "Don't tell on me. Okay?" She glanced toward the front door of the nursery, growing more anxious every moment. She was going to miss her chance.

But when she returned her gaze to Charlie, he was tugging his wagon down the sidewalk toward a boxy truck.

Lucy's heart sank... until he turned. "Well, are you coming, or aren't you?"

## CHAPTER 31—DELIA

By the time Meryl and Delia had finished their list and celebrated with a whole carafe of coffee, Delia was buzzing.

"I could tackle the entire front yard today. By the time Charlie gets back with the plants, there won't be a weed in sight. Mark my words!" she cried, as she hollered down the stairs to Meryl, snapping the left buckle of her overalls. Originally, she'd bought them for gardening the backyard of her Albatross Avenue home. Might as well get some use out of them now.

"Go for it," Meryl called back up. "I'll be in the downstairs bath. I need to finish painting."

Delia tied her hair back from her face and threw her sunglasses on, heading out into the warm sunshine without a care in the world. Bryant Astor himself could walk up to her and she wouldn't even notice, she was so over the moon.

She headed out, grabbing a hoe from the corner of the front porch, but just before she took to a particularly thorny briar patch at the base of the stoop, a lone figure drew her attention to the street.

Delia squinted through the sun rays, shielding her eyes as she made sense of the person there, on the sidewalk.

"Hello," she said cautiously. "Can I help you?" Delia rested the hoe against the porch and took a tentative step down the walk toward the woman.

The woman didn't answer, and once Delia's eyes adjusted to the light, she saw that it wasn't a woman at all.

It was just a girl.

"Oh, hello," Delia said, this time with a lighter way about her. Delight filled her two, simple words. She smiled and took three steps closer. "Are you—do you live nearby?"

The girl took a step backwards, north on the sidewalk, retreating the way she had come. "Sorry," she replied, her voice weak and sweet at once. Delia took her in—a white collared shirt tucked neatly into a khaki skirt. Knee-high socks and scuffed black shoes. Two braids, black as the night and slicked down severely into their ties. There was a darkness to her, overlaying the little voice. "I was just out for a walk. Didn't know there were people here."

"Don't apologize, please," Delia responded, making her way to the gate but stopping there. "I'm Delia. I just... well, I just moved in here. With my friend. Meryl Preston? Maybe you know her?"

The girl twitched.

Delia frowned. "Do you go to Shearwater?"

"I live there," she answered, her tone turning icy.

Delia knew this answer. She'd used it herself as a seventeen-year-old. No girl simply *went* to Shearwater.

They all lived there.

Delia smiled and tugged her sunglasses off. "I did, too. Once upon a time."

It was the sort of answer the girl couldn't ignore. She'd been about to turn, given her twisted stance, but she didn't. She froze and her shoulders squared on Delia. "You did?" Her face scrunched, and Delia pegged her age at about thirteen. Maybe twelve. Shearwater girls were typically younger than they looked. A reality that had haunted Delia until her first makeover at Le Spa des Oiseaux on the boardwalk.

Delia leaned against the gate post, the one she had just recently repaired and sanded down in preparation for paint. "Yep. My last year of high school. Mom died."

"They always do," the girl whispered back, worrying her fingertips together then running a hand down one of her braids. "Are you staying here?"

Delia frowned. "Well, yes. Like I said, we just moved in."

"Is it... *you* know. *Yours*?"

Unnerved by the bizarre question, Delia narrowed her gaze. "What do you mean?"

"Well, the last woman who moved in lived here, but it wasn't hers. The girls at my school say this place is—"

The low rumble of an oncoming truck tore the girl's focus from Delia. She whipped her head around and they both watched as Charlie's pick-up truck rolled toward them slowly. Light reflected off the windshield, hiding

Charlie from Delia's view. "Our handyman," she explained to the girl.

"I'd better go. Class starts soon."

"What's your name?" The question flew from Delia's lips before she could hold it in. Inexplicably, she felt a connection to this dark little child.

The girl looked at Delia as if she'd just threatened to kidnap her. "My friend—Meryl, the one who owns this place? She'll be one of your teachers come fall. That's why I ask. Mainly," she added earnestly.

The girl glanced at the house as if *it* was the tutor in question. "Oh," she answered. "I'm Bridget."

"Bridget," Delia answered. "I like that name." And she did, too. It was a fine name, for a fine-looking girl who probably didn't live a very fine life. Delia's heart panged in her chest. "Come over any time, Bridget."

"Why?" the girl asked, her brows falling harshly across the bridge of her nose, as if, again, Delia had said something untoward.

Delia glanced to where Charlie Peabody had just now parked then looked again at Bridget. "For any reason at all." She smiled, but by then, Bridget had swiveled away and was marching down the sidewalk. With a clearer view now, Delia saw the girl's socks sagging. Her skirt darker at the edges, as if they'd never once been through a good washing machine. The tail of her shirt wagged above her skirt like a sloppy tail. Most prominently, perhaps, the part in her braid was as crooked as Charlie Peabody's posture.

And still, Delia smiled broader.

Until she saw that Charlie Peabody was not alone.

## CHAPTER 32—MERYL

The back screendoor flapped open, and out stepped Delia, hands on her hips, triumphant. "We have visitors. Or... well, yes. Visitors, plural, I suppose."

Meryl paused in the middle of a brush stroke. She'd begun to paint the back porch, making slow progress—slower now that she was in it for the long haul. "Really?" she asked, straining to see beyond Delia and into the kitchen. "Who?"

"It's Lucy."

"Lucy and who? Her daughter?" Meryl cringed at an impending confrontation. What if the old woman's daughter had dragged her mother over here to chastise them all for sneaking around behind her back?

"Not *exactly*," Delia answered as Meryl wrapped the paintbrush in a wet rag and lay it over top of the can.

She followed her friend inside, through the kitchen and to the parlor, where Lucy's slight form appeared in the crook of the sofa. Standing with his cap in one hand and a thumb hooked along a suspender was Charlie.

"Well," Meryl announced, searching the area for someone else—a third person, a second visitor. Charlie no longer counted as a visitor. He was an employee, officially. "Charlie, hi. And—" Meryl rounded the sofa, meeting Lucy's gaze "—Lucy." She smiled then glanced at Delia for clarification.

A small mewing sound came from Lucy's vicinity, and Meryl's eyes flew to her, searching until they landed on a plastic chamber, of sorts, at Lucy's feet.

"My apologies for the intrusion," Lucy said, her voice throttled by some emotion. Grief. Fear. Something bad. Sad.

"It's not an intrusion," Meryl assured her, lowering to the edge of the sitting chair. "You're always welcome here. How's it going with your daughter?" Meryl flicked a look at the cat. Flashes of orange fur and a wet, pink nose shifted at the door of the little kennel.

Lucy adjusted the quilted handbag in her grasp and resituated herself in the seat. "Well, I come with a very grave request, I'm afraid. A plea, really. I had no one else to turn to—"

"You had me," Charlie cut in. If Meryl didn't know any better, she'd have thought Lucy shot a dagger of a stare at Charlie, but it left as quickly as it came, and a smile twitched across the old woman's mouth.

"Thank you, Mr. Peabody," she murmured.

"Charlie, please. Call me Charlie! How many times do I gotta..."

"Charlie, then," Lucy corrected. It was like watching a

little old couple squabble over where to eat dinner. An interaction Meryl regretted that she never got to see with her parents. Her own smile fell away, and she had to force a patient look onto her features.

"We're all ears, Lucy," Meryl said quietly. "If there's something you need, I'm sure we can help." This was God's honest truth, too. If there was one thing Meryl ought to do more of, it was to take after her parents. Had she been that way to begin with, who knew how life might have rolled? If she'd have said yes to their request for help, maybe they'd have driven more slowly. More carefully. Maybe her saying no spun her dad into a tizzy and caused him to be less cautious than he usually was? At the very least, if Meryl had said yes, she wouldn't feel sick to her stomach every time she thought of that final conversation with her mother. She shook her head slightly, to herself, out of notice of Lucy and the others.

Lucy cleared her throat, a soft rattling paving the way for whatever favor she needed. "You see, my daughter and son-in-law were to find a good home for Fiona here." Lucy indicated the kennel and the audibly purring feline. "I found out today that the poor thing has been on death row at the Farm, for goodness' sake." She shook her head and clicked her tongue almost violently. "Thankfully, Charlie here found me and drove me over there, and we managed to talk the manager into letting me reclaim her."

"Oh, Lucy," Delia trilled from next to Meryl, "what a hard morning you must have had. You've got to be exhausted."

Lucy nodded wearily. "I am, and I'm sure Charlie here

is tired, too. Tired of putting up with me, I'm sure." Meryl watched as Lucy lifted a silver eyebrow at the old man, and—again—if she didn't know any better, she'd have thought Charlie Peabody *winked* at Lucy. Winked!

"Not a lick," Charlie assured everyone heartily. "In fact, soon as this matter here is settled, I'll drive Miss Lucy wherever she sees fit to go. After that, I'll return promptly and finish the day's work here. Then, back to G.O. I go!"

"Be that as it may," Lucy went on, "I've got to find a home for Fiona. They can't just *put her down*. If I had known my daughter was going to drop her off at the Farm, I'd never have agreed to leave my house on First Street. So here I am, doing the one thing I asked Marcia to do."

Meryl's heart panged for Lucy. And for Marcia, too. It was a rotten thing to do to her mother—she could have worked harder to secure a placement, no doubt. But Meryl knew that sometimes, what was best for a human compromised what might be best for her pet. It was a hard spot. She eyed Lucy's wrist brace and wondered what else had transpired to build a road between the old woman's family home and her entrance into Golden Oaks.

"Asking us to help you find a home for your cat?" Meryl asked.

"Like I said," Lucy answered, "I'm not sure who else to turn to. The shelter here doesn't make placements. Just euthanizations." Lucy's voice was filled with heartache and sadness, and Meryl easily agreed with Lucy, despite not even knowing Marcia.

"You turn to us. We take her," Meryl said without a second thought. "We'll take Fiona," Meryl repeated for emphasis. She stood and stepped to the kennel, crouching and curling her fingers around the wiry spindles. Fiona mewed appreciatively. Meryl looked up at Lucy, whose mouth had fallen open. "Until you can take her back, of course."

Lucy's mouth worked closed then open again. Meryl and Delia exchanged a knowing look, and Delia spoke next. "Lucy, if Fiona is so special to you, you should live somewhere where she can live, too."

"That's right, Lucy," Meryl agreed.

"No, no. I—I need the help. That's one thing Marcia and I can agree on. I can't be alone."

"What about an apartment? You'd keep your freedom but live close to others. That could work, right? Something on the first floor?" Meryl suggested. She found herself rejuvenated by counseling this sweet old woman. Almost as rejuvenated as she'd felt when she'd gone out on a limb and applied at Shearwater. Brief thoughts of John Quinn filtered in and out of her brain, and she made a quick mental note to bake him cookies as a special thank you. Then, she gave it a second thought and realized that might be a little too much.

Lucy shrugged. "I could do that, perhaps," she agreed. "I like Golden Oaks well enough." Lucy looked at Charlie who appeared to be on the brink of falling asleep standing up, his eyes drooping and chin heavy. "But I love Fiona more. It kills me to know where she was. What my daughter thought was right—well, it was wrong. *She* was wrong."

"Would you like for us to call her? Maybe we just need to see if she would reconsider taking Fiona in?" Delia offered.

Lucy shook her head miserably. "Chris—that's Marcia's husband—he's deathly allergic. Even packing my house put him out. He coughed half the while and the other half complained about how his throat was clenching up on him."

"That does sound like a bad effect," Charlie chimed in, reawakened by something or other. "I once got stung by a bee. Damn near killed me. I can relate to this young man you speak of."

Lucy pressed her mouth into a line and shook her head once more. "It's not Chris I blame. I just wish my daughter had more energy than to drop Fiona off at the Farm like an old teddy bear. She had enough energy to come and pick me up for a day at the boardwalk. She could have spent that time putting up posters or calling the paper and placing an ad." Lucy's brow line fell, and her mouth froze. "Then again, I s'pose I had time to do any one of those things myself." She lifted her eyes to Meryl. "I wrote my advertisement for a roommate, you know."

Meryl smiled at her. "I know, Lucy. I know you did. And you could have done an ad for Fiona, too. But then, that's hard, isn't it? Maybe it was hard for Marcia?"

"Maybe," Lucy allowed. "Either way, either Fiona and I are out of a home, or just Fiona, unless I can find somewhere for her."

"Lucy, Fiona can live here. But—" she set her jaw, ignoring her compulsion to look at Delia for permission about what she was going to offer next. She already had a clear sense of where Delia might fall on the matter. And Meryl also knew that this may be another opportunity for Delia. A way to contribute. To do the thing she so wanted to do—*work*. "Lucy," Meryl went on, lowering to her knees in front of the old woman as she held her hand near Fiona's face, the cat feeling her out with her bristly whiskers. "Why don't you stay, too?"

## CHAPTER 33—LUCY

She couldn't stay at the Mill River House. She simply could not.

But then, there was this Charlie character sort of watching from the shadows. For some reason inexplicable to Lucy, she felt that she needed to prove something to *him*, a perfect stranger. Then again, she was sitting in a houseful of strangers, asking them for help with Fiona.

This really was the end of the line, when an old woman had to take drastic measures just for the sake of a house cat.

Lucy looked down at Fiona, who'd begun purring under Meryl's attention.

"If you'd be willing to take Fiona, that's all the help I need. I'd be indebted to you forever. But I won't stay. Couldn't do that to you fine ladies. After all, you're selling, right?"

Meryl looked up at her from her position on the floor next to Fiona. "Actually, no. Some events have transpired, and it turns out we're staying. Delia will rent a room—

just like you could—and I'm going to teach at Shearwater, come fall." She smiled. "There are some details to work out yet. I have to figure out a plan for my condo in Newark—that's where I'm from, you see—and my job there. But, Lucy, we'll be here in Gull's Landing from now until who knows when? We have the space. We'd love your company."

Lucy worked her mouth as her brain took in all this information.

"I came here originally because I was looking for a room to rent, yes. And when I discovered that 12 Mill River Road really could be up for grabs, I had to see it for myself. Then I came here, and sure enough you two waffled about the fate of this old place. Well," she grabbed her cane and tamped it down onto the thick oriental rug, "I'm only here now to buy time for my girl there. Fiona, I mean. As for me, I'll be at Golden Oaks until the end, no doubt. But I can find a long-term home for Fiona soon. I'm sure I can. And maybe my daughter will even help this time. But to hear you are staying for the long haul—" Lucy shook her head and clicked her tongue "—why, it's unimaginable, frankly."

Charlie chuckled in the corner and Lucy flashed a glance at him. He clearly wasn't from around here. He didn't know what had gone on at 12 Mill River Road. He didn't know what made it a famous house so many years ago. Or, infamous, as the case may be. And clearly neither did these two naive ladies, with their scheme to turn the place into a veritable brothel. Lucy was curious about it, sure. She wasn't *interested*, though.

Then again... whatever happened to her hope for freedom?

Well, maybe this was the sign she needed. Maybe freedom had nothing to do with living on one's own.

Maybe, freedom was simply sailing into the sunset, unbothered by the dramatic histories of the past. Unaffected by true tragedy, be it personal or not.

Maybe Lucy ought to thank her lucky stars.

"Charlie, I'm ready to return to G.O.," she declared, using his pet name for the place.

Charlie nodded once. "Ladies, might I make a quick errand before returning for my day?"

Lucy watched as Meryl pushed up from the sofa and studied her friend. At last, she turned to Charlie. "Go on, Charlie." Then, she looked at Lucy. "You have an open invitation here, you know."

"Just keep my girl safe for me for a little while. I'll be in touch as soon as I find someone who wants her." Lucy's eyes pricked with tears, but instead of bidding Fiona farewell and sobbing like a schoolgirl, she made her way to the door. I'll be back soon, God willing."

THE RIDE back to Golden Oaks was worse than the first time she went there. Sitting so close to this Charlie gentleman set Lucy's nerves on fire. Then there was Fiona, left again at some strange place. This one as bad as the Farm in some ways. But better, too. After all, just because 12 Mill River Road had a dark history didn't mean that its current residents were trouble. If anyone was trouble, clearly it was Lucy.

And *in* trouble she would be, the minute she stepped foot back in Golden Oaks.

Charlie opened the front door for Lucy, and Nurse Ratched was there, just inside of the door, waiting like a vulture.

"You two, in the manager's office. *Now*."

Lucy and Charlie shared a confused look before they followed the orderly into the spacious room down the hall beyond the front desk.

Lucy had only ever spoken with the Golden Oaks manager once, after her first tour. To talk to him a second time felt like being called into the principal's office. Maybe worse.

Most certainly worse, in fact.

"Miss Spaur. Mr. Peabody. I prefer not to pry into the business of our residents—or our employees, for that matter." He steepled his hands as he spoke, looking at each one of them as they sat across from him. "But might I inquire as to where you've been?"

To Lucy, this was not a question of propriety, and she answered without hesitation. "At a friend's house in the countryside, tending to a personal custody matter."

The manager blinked and pulled his spectacles half an inch lower along his nose. "Custody matter?" Then he shook his head. "Your excursion attendant and driver waited an *hour* for you at The Greenery. Looked for you, Miss Spaur, for one entire *hour* before calling here. We were on the cusp of calling the police. Your daughter is on her way."

"Marcia?" Lucy asked, steeling herself for an explosion from the office door at any moment. "Oh, heavens. I was with my friends! Charlie gave me a ride."

"And that brings me to another concern," the manager went on.

Lucy could practically feel Charlie trembling beside her, though she was still bewildered over it all.

"This is a sensitive point, and it is with great discomfort that I must remind you both that we strictly prohibit staff from fraternizing with residents. And vice versa, to be frank."

Horrified at his implication, Lucy froze. She could feel Charlie do the same.

The manager went on. "It's a one-strike rule we adhere to. Miss Spaur, our concern lies in the power and age imbalance, you see. Though Mr. Peabody is not among our youngest employees, it was highly indecent of him—"

Lucy interrupted fiercely. "Pardon me, but it was *I* who took advantage of Mr. Peabody's kind offer. And as for fraternizing—"

"I'm very sorry, sir," Charlie cut in himself, his head lowered. Lucy became all too aware of his circumstances. Despite Charlie's easy way and confident demeanor, he was a very low man on the totem pole. "It won't happen again, I assure you."

"I know it won't happen again," the manager went on, "Because today will be your last—"

"What?" Lucy snapped, something in her unwinding and free-falling through the atmosphere as she exploded at the manager. "You're going to fire him? My *fiancé*?!"

Lucy cried, shocking even herself at the off-the-cuff lie. It was instinctive. She had to protect poor, innocent Charlie. He had helped her. Now, it was her chance to think quickly on her feet and return the favor.

The manager and Charlie both stared at her in equal measurements of confusion and shock.

Charlie lowered his voice. "Lucy," he warned.

"That's right. Before I even came to Golden Oaks the first time, Charlie Peabody proposed marriage to me. We met at our friend's house, you see. Out on Mill River Road. I accepted, you understand. My residency here has nothing to do with it, but you should know that if you fire him, you *lose* me. For good. And that's not all. You lose those friends of mine who might one day consider checking themselves into this dingy old place, too!"

"I beg your pardon," the manager struggled to say. "You two are—betrothed?"

"Tell him, Charlie—tell him that a soon-to-be married couple has every right to enjoy the morning together, regardless of employment this or residency that."

Charlie simply shook his head, despite the guilt-stricken look on his face.

Lucy pursed her lips. "Now, if you'll excuse us back to our own business, I won't report you to the proper authorities for discrimination, Mr. *Man*," she snapped and stood up, leaving no room for a reply.

Charlie fumbled to follow her to the door, and the manager remained at his desk, entirely stupefied and rightly so.

But Lucy didn't care.

Charlie walked her back to her room, and it was time to play the role.

He dropped his voice at her door. "What do I do now?" he asked.

Lucy flashed a glance down the hall only to see the manager appear from his office and search for them, his eyes landing squarely on their figures not a hundred yards down.

She looked back at Charlie. "Kiss me, you fool," she said.

And, to her own astonishment, he did.

## CHAPTER 34—DELIA

"Did you know that Charlie lives at the Y?" Delia asked Meryl as they sat on the front porch. Delia petting Fiona who sunbathed across her lap, purring contentedly.

"The Y? As in the YMCA?" Meryl asked, frowning. "Like, alone?"

"Maybe he shares a room there. I'm not sure. We spoke a little the other day. I feel bad for him."

Meryl took a sip of her drink. They'd start back on yard work in a short while, but until Charlie returned, it was break time. "Why? He seems happy enough. Especially chauffeuring Lucy Spaur around town. They'd make an adorable couple. Feisty Lucy with the cane that's nearly her height and her pretty white hair. That attitude —she cracks me up, Delia. I hope I'm half that brazen at her age."

"They only just met at Golden Oaks. Charlie talked all about it. He wants to live there. It's his dream, I guess."

"What?" Meryl asked, "He can't afford to?"

Delia shook her head. "I'm sure not. Not if he's living at the Y. I think he's been doing odd jobs for a long, long time. Do you know he's worked here before?"

"Here?" Meryl cut a sidelong glance at her. "Like, when this place belonged to my grandparents or something?"

Delia thought about what he'd said then shrugged. "I'm not sure. He just said he was familiar with the property. Had been around before."

"Was he ever married?"

"Actually, I don't think so. But he alluded to a significant other." She looked at Meryl. "Almost like a secret girlfriend."

Meryl smirked. "Could it have been Lucy all along?"

Delia instantly shook her head, "No, I don't think so. He made a big to-do about being taken with her. It was sweet." Delia then lifted her chin out toward the street. "Speaking of which, John Quinn."

"What about him?" Meryl looked away, but the smile on her face said it all.

"You tell me," Delia prodded gently. "You two seemed to… hit it off?"

"Professionally, sure," Meryl answered, her tone mild. "He's in education. I'm in education. Now we have a shared geographic area."

"'Shared geographic area?'" Delia laughed. "He's your neighbor."

"My neighbor," Meryl echoed wistfully.

"Your attractive neighbor who shares your professional interests."

Meryl shot her a look. "I didn't know the school even

had a head*master* before we walked over there. So, if you're accusing me of basing my decision on the fact that John Quinn just so *happens* to be good looking, then you're barking up the wrong tree."

Delia raised her hands in surrender. "I'm not implying anything. Or accusing. I'm just... curious. Mainly because I wonder how that old place is doing. If they've changed their rotten ways. I saw a girl from there this morning."

"A student?"

"Ward. Student. Whatever you want to call her. She was out for a walk, and I think I spooked her."

"Did she look rotten? Was the school rotten when you went there?"

Delia just shook her head. "It's a boarding school for foster girls. Troubled girls. Orphans. What do you expect? Even a good-looking headmaster isn't going to make much of a difference in those girls' lives."

Meryl frowned at her. "Did you always have that opinion of teachers?"

Blinking, Delia felt a little embarrassed. "Look, Meryl, my life now is *nothing* like my life back then. My mom and I—we were poor. Really poor. Then she died, and I was beyond poor. I was homeless. The fact that someone got me into Shearwater was supposed to be a miracle, but that place was worse than living under the boardwalk would have been. It's obviously changed now, but back then the *girls* made the rules. They ran the school."

"They made the rules, huh? And a bunch of kids made the rule not to go down to the house at the other end of the street?" Meryl scoffed. "Makes a lot of sense."

But Delia just shrugged. "That's how it works for hard kids. There *are* rules. They just may not be logical to adults. Anyway, I felt bad for her."

"For who?" Meryl asked.

"The little girl who came along. Bridget. She had to be young. Thirteen at the most. Reminded me of... well, of no one. And that was the sad thing."

## CHAPTER 35—MERYL

Charlie did not return alone.

With him was Lucy. Driving in a car behind him, a younger woman and man, their faces hidden by the glare off their windshield.

Meryl moved to the gate at the front of the yard. Charlie hopped out, or moved out of the truck in such a way as a spry oldster could. He then cornered the hood and opened the passenger door before holding out his hand and helping a victorious-looking Lucy down from her seat.

Meryl looked over her shoulder at Delia, who carried Fiona to join her at the gate. "She's back," Meryl said, stating the obvious.

"And with whom?" Delia asked, craning her neck around the truck.

"Hello, Lucy!" Meryl called out, opening the gate and striding to her to take her quilted bag from Charlie so that he could assist Lucy down the walk.

"Meryl," Lucy answered. "Delia," she added. "I had to

come back here, because there was a confrontation at Golden Oaks, you see."

"A confrontation?" Meryl looked over to the people getting out of their car. Were these Golden Oaks folks?

"Hi," the woman from the car announced her presence on the sidewalk as she joined Lucy with a gentle grip under her elbow. "I'm Marcia. This is my husband, Chris," she gestured back to the man standing awkwardly in the distance. "I'm so sorry we're here to bother you, but my mother *insisted* we come here."

"I'll explain everything over coffee," Lucy declared, pointing inside. "If that suits you, Meryl and Delia?"

Meryl grinned and nodded. "Of course. Of *course*. Everyone, come right in."

"I'll put coffee on," Delia offered as they shuffled along the walk and through the gate, up the footpath and through the front door of 12 Mill River Road.

A place that was fast becoming more than an abandoned house. More than a house, even.

A place that was becoming... *something*.

ONCE EVERYONE WAS in the parlor, seated and sipping as contentedly as possible, Meryl raised the question on everyone's minds. "Lucy, you mentioned... a confrontation?"

Lucy didn't hesitate to reply. With Fiona purring softly on her lap, she held court there as though she was always somehow connected to that house on 12 Mill River Road.

"You see, we had an outing—the Golden Oaks bus took us to the nursery. There, I bumped into Charlie, here." She smiled at him and he at her. Meryl glanced at Marcia who met her gaze and smirked. "Anyway," Lucy went on, "I never went to the nursery to browse ferns. I went on the reasonable assumption that they'd take me just up the road to the Farm, naturally."

"Mother," Marcia cut in. She flushed and lowered her coffee. "Everyone, I want to interject in our defense."

Lucy shook her head but then answered, "No one is here to condemn you, Marcia."

"My husband is allergic to cats," Marcia continued defensively. "Even so, he and I discussed seriously keeping Fiona in a spare room in our house or the like. In the end, my *mother* agreed for us to find a new home for her. I put a notice in the paper and went to the Farm, because, well, that's where you *go* for this sort of thing." She was frazzled to the max, and Meryl had only to nod sympathetically for her to finish her explanation. "The people there assured me they'd keep Fiona on as an adoptee candidate and actively advertise her. They said she'd go quickly and to the best home, because she was well cared for."

"And beautiful," Delia added.

Lucy smiled at her. "Thank you, Delia. Well, anyway, I did not realize the extent to which Marcia had gone. But nonetheless, I intended to see to my cat." Lucy's face broke. "I know I sound pathetic," she sobbed quietly.

"Oh, Mom." Marcia shifted down the sofa and wrapped an arm around Lucy. She glanced at Meryl and then Delia. "I am so sorry we've drawn you into this. I think my mother—she's going through a transition. At my hands, I know. I think she's—"

"Well, she's lonely as hell!" Charlie declared.

All eyes flew to the man standing crookedly against the far wall. An outsider who'd turned insider. Meryl's chest clenched at his claim.

Lucy buried her face in her hands. "I didn't finish my story," she said through a trembling voice.

Marcia rubbed her back. "Go ahead, Mom. Then we need to get going. We've taken up enough of these kind ladies' time."

Lucy took a breath. "Charlie did take me to the Farm, where I got Fiona, as you all know."

Meryl and Delia nodded.

"When he took me back to Golden Oaks, the manager confronted us." Her mouth twisted and she repositioned Fiona on her lap. "He accused us of indecent behavior, if you can imagine that."

Chris, who'd hung back by the staircase, chuckled, and it was hard not to join him.

Marcia snapped her fingers at her husband and shot him a severe look.

"Lucy, here, saved my chops," Charlie added gruffly. "That manager was going to give me the boot. And I've been doing odd jobs at G.O. for goldarn near twenty years. Here and there."

Meryl was losing track. She held up a hand. "Now, just a minute. The manager accused you two of something indecent, and then he threatened to, what? Fire Charlie?"

"That's right. So I told him there was nothing indecent between us because we were already engaged. Then I told him if he was going to make a fuss about it, I'd move right out of there and warn all my friends never to set foot inside!" Lucy shifted and huffed, and again Chris laughed from behind them all.

"I have to say," Marcia interjected, "I'm pretty impressed with it all."

"Well, anyway, the manager didn't touch us after that, but we had to, well, play along." Charlie grinned sheepishly.

Delia asked, "And the manager just... believed all this?"

Lucy shrugged. "Younger folks go one of two ways. Either they're afraid of us geezers or scornful. I think the manager was both, but he prizes his institution more than its rules, naturally."

"But now you're here?" Meryl asked gently. "Come to get Fiona back?"

"Mom is going to live with us. As for Fiona, like I said —the Farm can find a placement for her. Probably one where Mom can visit. Isn't that right, Chris?"

"That's right," he said.

Meryl's shoulders lifted and fell. "Well, that's a shame, then."

Delia shared a glance with her. "I agree. Fiona seems to get along nicely here."

"And, Delia and I were looking forward to finding a second tenant," Meryl added.

"A second tenant?" Marcia looked back and forth between Delia and Meryl. "Where? *Here*? Are you—are you turning this place into a boardinghouse?"

Meryl smiled, her eyes twinkling. "Something like that."

But Delia shook her head. "Not a boardinghouse. I've already done the boardinghouse thing, except it was a boarding *school*."

Meryl gave her a kind look. "Right. We aren't about to call it a boardinghouse."

Lucy interjected. She glanced up along the walls warily. "Maybe you should call it a *haunted* house."

## CHAPTER 36—LUCY

"Haunted?" Meryl and Delia asked together.

Fiona mewed irritably.

"Haunted, Mom?" Marcia asked, too.

Charlie sniffled in the corner and Lucy thought, briefly, that maybe he *was* in on Gull's Landing's dirty little secret. Maybe he knew something.

Or maybe there was a second secret about 12 Mill River Road. A secret to which even Lucy wasn't privy.

"Before Marcia was born, I worked just down the street from here," Lucy revealed, relishing the attention of the others.

"At Shearwater, you mean?" Delia asked. "What year? I *went* to Shearwater."

Lucy studied Delia then glanced at Marcia. The two were closer in age than she realized, perhaps. But still, Delia came later.

"Before your time, too, I'd imagine. When I was much, *much* younger. Just a girl, really."

"I didn't know you worked at Shearwater, Mom," Marcia pointed out.

"It was a bad year. A year I don't like to go back to. And probably the reason your parents, Meryl, never did much with this place."

Meryl's mouth fell open. "You knew my mother?"

"No," Lucy answered. "Gladys Preston? No. Not her parents, either. We were townies. The Stevers were country folk. Those kids ran barefoot in the woods. Rarely came to town or to the shore, even. Much too busy to enjoy life, those folks."

A sadness shaped Meryl's eyes. They crinkled at the edges. "Oh. That... makes sense, I suppose."

"Anyway," Lucy went on. "After the Stevers were long gone and the house had fallen into Gladys' ownership, there was a tragedy here, supposedly."

"Tragedy?" Marcia asked. "I never heard about any tragedy."

"It was all very hush-hush," Lucy confirmed. "The school didn't want a lawsuit. Neither did the property owners."

"You mean my grandparents?" Meryl asked.

Lucy shrugged. "Either they or your parents. Like I said, I'm not entirely sure who kept this place by then."

"So, what happened?" Charlie asked, outing himself as being in the dark, after all.

"Those days were different. The headmaster of Shearwater didn't know how to handle girls. Especially rough ones. The ones that were always searching. And they were, too. When I worked there as a tutor, those girls wouldn't stay in a seat for longer than five minutes. They crawled around this town like vermin."

"Vermin," Delia whispered.

"I'm sorry." Lucy looked at her, ashamed. "I didn't mean—"

"No, it's just—I know what you mean. When I was there, it was just that way. Except there was something... something off. The roaming was... reigned in. But not by the faculty, mind you. By the girls themselves. There was a code. A strict code amongst the girls. Like something had... *happened*. Even just this morning, it was very odd to see that girl walk down here."

"A girl from the school?" Lucy inquired.

"Yes. Bridget. A pretty, dark little thing. She was just on a walk, wandering around. A bit spooked, perhaps."

"Maybe the word got out," Lucy suggested.

"What word, Mom? What *happened*?"

"When I worked there," Lucy went on gravely, "the girls would sneak out and over to this place. This house. Right here." Lucy waved her hands around wildly.

"That's no surprise," Meryl added stuffily. "If a vagrant was living here, then it makes sense that teenagers would use it as a hangout."

"She wasn't a vagrant," Charlie croaked.

Lucy's gaze flew to Charlie. "Who?"

Meryl answered by way of a question. "The woman who was found in here just a couple weeks ago? The homeless woman?"

He nodded soberly. "She was... she wasn't a vagrant. We, um—" his voice cracked, and he ran a hand over his eyes. "I've got to go. I can't... I can't... Miss Preston, I'm very sorry. We—I—"

Lucy's hand flew to her mouth. "That woman who died? Oh, Charlie. She was your—"

Delia chimed in. "She was your wife?"

## CHAPTER 37—DELIA

"Common law," Charlie admitted. "We had no place to go. Not together. We stayed on here. We tended the place best we could. Couldn't do much with the yard or else we'd draw attention to ourselves, naturally," he added.

"Why didn't you go to the funeral? Or before that—why didn't you go to the police? Claim her?"

"Because what we did was illegal," he admitted. "Squatting here like criminals. And what's more, it wouldn't have mattered. I was afraid I'd be let go from Golden Oaks, and then what? I'd really be in trouble. I just took up with the Y soon as it happened."

"Oh, Charlie," Delia murmured. Her heart broke for him. Here was this shell of a man, a hard-working, strong and sinewy old man who never quit. And yet, he was around. Living amongst those in Gull's Landing, without help. Without charity. Without much of anything, except for someone to love.

And then she died. And he couldn't even claim her. At least, he didn't want to.

Delia, of all people, sympathized with him. She sympathized with the poor man on so many levels. On losing the love of his life. On having no place to call home. On worrying where to go next. What to do. Who to be, even. And here he was, under the microscope of all those past failures. On the brink of exposure. Persecution, perhaps.

Delia looked at Meryl, willing into her friend to act on all the sympathy and compassion that surely Meryl had to possess.

"You were... you were *living* here?" Meryl asked. Disgust colored her tone, but Delia could see she was trying hard to digest the information, rather than regurgitate it.

Charlie pushed off of the wall and bowed his head. "I'll just go on, now," he said, looking craggier than ever. "I'm sorry for fooling all of you. I never meant harm. I swear to that."

"You didn't harm anyone, Charlie," Lucy pointed out. "Just, oh, heavens." She looked at Delia then Meryl, who seemed to carry the most power at the moment, having been the owner of the place. "I can top that story, anyway," Lucy declared. "You'll see. What Charlie and his sweetheart did here will seem like an act of salvation. Like a good thing."

"What is your story, Lucy?" Meryl asked. Delia could hear in her voice a moral struggle, a desire to see the best in her new friends. To help. To—maybe—be more like her parents than she really wanted to be.

Chris had moved to the back of the sofa, listening as acutely as possible. Delia and Meryl were frozen on their sitting chairs. Charlie hovered awkwardly at the invisible threshold between the parlor and the foyer. On his way out. Unsure. Scared and sad and everything in between, the poor thing.

"Well," Lucy went on. "To put it plainly, an orphan girl died here."

## CHAPTER 38—MERYL

A collective gasp rippled across the room.

Meryl, perhaps the most shocked of all, had a million questions. Right away. "Who was she? Did my mom and dad know? My grandparents?"

"Gladys Preston knew. And your father must have as well. The school privately sued them for negligence. The house was deemed an attractive nuisance, considering both its condition and its location so near to the orphanage." Lucy's mouth sealed into a firm line. She seemed to know what she was talking about. "I thought you had an inkling."

"How much did they sue for? What year was this? Did they pay? How did she *die*?" Suddenly, Charlie's confession paled in comparison. Lucy was right. Nothing could compare to the tragedy of a child.

Not vagrancy. Not homelessness.

Nothing.

"I don't know the details, but I know that they did pay the school. Whatever the amount was, they paid it and then some, I do believe. As for the girl, she was with others. They dared her, I think." Lucy's eyes grew smaller as she appeared to remember. "Yes. That was it. A whole group of them broke in and dared her to stay the night. When she didn't come back the next morning, the girls returned to see if she had made good on the dare."

Delia looked like she might sob. "What happened to her?"

"They found her in the basement. The wood was rotten in one of the first-floor rooms. She fell through and broke her neck, probably."

Silence swept the parlor.

Images of the dolls on the hearth crossed through Meryl's mind like a reel of nightmares. The dark, different patch of wood. But, still, Meryl shook her head. "No," she said confidently.

"What do you mean *no*?" Delia asked, looking sick to her stomach.

"There's no basement. You know that, Delia. We've cleaned this house top to bottom. No basement."

"Maybe she fell from the second floor to the first?" Delia offered, staring meaningfully at Lucy.

"Oh, no. It was the basement. I'm sure of it." Lucy shifted in her seat.

"How can you be sure? If there is no basement, then that wasn't it. Clearly. Are you certain she died here? Is this perhaps one of those small-town rumors that get mixed up over the years?" As the ideas flew from Meryl's mouth, she thought about her parents. Their constant scramble to give, give, give. To help, help, help. And then, at last, Viola's revelation that they were in up to their eyeballs in debt. Despite having it all, they had, in truth, nothing.

"There's a basement, all right," Charlie pointed out. "What do you think that exterior door leads to?"

"It's a... a shed. A crawlspace," Meryl answered. "It goes nowhere. It's a small little alcove, nothing more. And anyway, how would you know if it was something more? You haven't been around that long, surely." Her words dripped with acid, even though she liked Charlie. She was confused. Confused about her decision to stay in a house like that, with people like this.

Charlie cleared his throat. "The brick is fresh, Miss Preston. Fresh as the first snow. Compared to the rest of this house, which was built a century ago, at least. That brick is just decades old." He blinked. "I always knew there was something beyond that wall."

"And, what?" Meryl asked, "They had a basement but had to go outside to get in there? Makes no sense." She was adamant. Adamant that the house she was ready to call home wasn't horrifying. Or haunted, as Lucy suggested. All these trickling truths arrested her in her recent plans. Maybe she wouldn't sell her condo or quit her job. Maybe she wouldn't tutor down the street for the needy girls and the handsome headmaster and the small town from *hell*.

Chris put his hand on the door beneath the staircase. "Where does this lead?" he asked innocently.

Meryl shot up from her seat and rounded the sofa to join him. "It's another alcove." She looked back urgently to the others, but Lucy sat stolidly. Her face impassive. The truth evident in her eyes. Delia's expression was more pained. Charlie's too. Marcia stood and joined Meryl and Chris.

"Open it. Let's look," she offered.

Chris moved out of the way, and Meryl opened the door with a jerking tug. Inside sat the same warm red brick wall that had stood out to her when she first came. How it didn't match the rest of the house. How the cement wasn't worn away in the seams and the whole facade of it stood disparately from everything else about the old, creaking wooden house.

"Why would they do this?" Meryl asked. "Okay, so if a girl did die by sneaking in here, I mean that's awful. It is. But it wasn't my parents' fault. Or my grandparents'. Why cover it up?"

"They tried to sell it," Lucy answered. "But to sell it, they felt like they had to hide the history. Or rather, they had to keep the history hidden. Not that there was anything to find there after the clean-up, but I suppose it was more of a psychological act. One of a guilty conscience, to brick it all in. God forbid another girl wander over and get hurt in the basement. Truthfully, I'm surprised they didn't board this place up at the very least, but I suppose that wouldn't do either—couldn't sell a boarded-up place."

"It didn't make news?" Meryl was floored by all of this. But, at the same time, it made perfect sense. She longed to call Viola and throttle the woman into telling her version of the story. But something deep down told Meryl that even Viola didn't know.

As if to confirm Meryl's sinking feeling, Delia answered quietly. "News about the orphanage has always died off well in advance before making it to the public. And what *does* make it that far is marked as hearsay. Gossip. Fodder for an institution on the fringe of society—quite literally. Shearwater girls are invisible when they go into that place, and that's how they stay. Even once they're out."

"So, Lucy's right," Meryl replied coolly. Miserably. "This isn't a boardinghouse." She glanced at Delia, a sad smile flickering across her mouth. "And it's certainly not a country club."

Charlie cleared his throat. He was near the door now, scooching inch by inch until he was about to disappear into the day. Back to the Y. Maybe back to his job at G.O. or some other blue collar, low-paying gig that would provide him enough money to get by. Something that would keep him, too, invisible. Then, just as he was close enough to the door to make his escape, he said, "It's not a haunted house, either."

Meryl held her hand up, as if to stop him. "What do you mean?"

A wistful smile pushed his sagging cheeks back into apples and he looked over at Lucy, there on the sofa. Fiona had leapt up some minutes ago and was now scampering after some unseen point of interest. A spider or a shadow, invisible to everyone except Fiona. "People have lived here and explored here. They've snuck in and out and spent the best days of their lives here."

"And the worst," Meryl responded, thinking back to the early days when the pain of losing her parents was so great that she wanted nothing to do with it. Or them, even. And now here she was, desperate for every last detail. "Even my own parents, it seems, couldn't escape the heartache. It wasn't me they were running from. It wasn't even the bills, either. It was, like Lucy said, guilt." Meryl remained thoughtful for a moment. Then she added, "I bet people think they want to live in a house like this. This great, big, beautiful place—there is room for everyone here. But in the end, it isn't the dream locale one might hope for."

"Sounds a lot like The Landing, come to think of it," Delia added, mischief streaking her face.

Lucy added after a chuckle, "You mean a country club?"

Delia smiled broadly. "That's *exactly* what I mean. Not just any country club, though. This place could be *our* country club. *The* Country Club."

# EPILOGUE

And a country club, they became. In a sense. By Christmas of the following year, 12 Mill River Road buzzed with holiday cheer. And with life. Old and young.

Once Meryl started working at Shearwater, she came to find that John Quinn's qualities didn't end with a thick head of dark hair and kind green eyes. Oh, no. He intended to turn Shearwater into as safe and proper an institution as it could possibly be, while still serving those less fortunate girls of the area.

His rates of high school graduation for the older girls outpaced even those of Wildwood's and Ocean City's various boarding schools—girls' only, boys' only, and the few co-ed institutions.

One thing turned into another, and Meryl signed on for a second year at Shearwater. A mutual interest between Meryl and John took hold.

Over time, she had started inviting John to dinner. It was in these early courting experiences between Meryl and John that Delia came to know more and more about the dark-haired girl called Bridget. In fact, she was far younger than Delia had thought. Nine, not thirteen. Which meant she was just halfway through her stay at Shearwater, by all accounts.

As she became friendlier with her tutor, Miss Preston, Bridget made regular walks past the old house at 12 Mill River Road. She'd slow down when she saw Delia outside planting flowers or reading a book. Sometimes, she'd stop and help Lucy fiddle with the mailbox until she could work it open, carrying letters inside for the old woman. Once or twice, she even helped Charlie, 12 Mill River Road's lone male tenant, take out a trash bag or two.

Finally, after weeks and weeks of little moments between Bridget and the motley residents of 12 Mill River Road, Delia dug into Bridget's history. With John's help, she managed to take Bridget in as a long-term foster. With dead parents and no other family to speak of, it was natural that Delia and Bridget bonded as foster mother and foster daughter, although they didn't yet use those titles. Adoption was an option, but a pricey one, it turned out. Well, it wouldn't have been pricey when Delia was still living on Albatross Avenue and throwing money into the wind with Bryant.

But now any amount of money was too much money. Anyway, adoption or not, Delia grew to love Bridget as her own, and Bridget seemed to love Delia, too. Enough so that Bridget had moved in by the end of that first full year.

And that brought the total in the house to five. Five full-time residents. And though Delia was back to living in a crowded boarding-style house, it surely didn't feel like that. It felt like something. Like a soft place to fall. Like what she would have hoped to see The Landing become, when she was still the president of the HOA.

So, over dinner on that chilly Christmas night, after Lucy gave the blessing, Meryl made a toast.

"To our patchwork group, friends forever."

"To us," Charlie agreed.

"And to the Prestons," Delia added. "May they rest in peace knowing that everything turned out okay here."

And it had. Though it was difficult to get all the correct information, Meryl and Aunt Viola had pieced together the truth. That Lucy's memory was correct and that, indeed, the secretive lawsuit remained buried beneath the layers of indifference most of the public held when it came to the pitiful girls' school and its sad wards. It was also true that they had paid all they had, leveraging one income property over another where they could, to try and get ahead eventually. But mainly, they lived their lives running from their guilt and chasing after some form of forgiveness. Meryl did what she could to achieve that for them. First, by committing to her stay at 12 Mill River Road, and second, by staying on at Shearwater and giving the job her all.

Christmas dinner was nothing short of divine. They enjoyed Lucy's famous lemon chicken and Bridget's much-improved rendition of Delia's recipe for gooey double-fudge brownies. After dinner, the group of eight —John, Marcia, and Chris had joined them, of course— retired together to the parlor, where Charlie stoked a roaring red fire and Fiona purred loudly from her special nook beneath the staircase.

Once the flames lapped wildly inside of the iron grates, Charlie settled onto the sofa with Lucy, where together they sipped hot cocoa from matching mugs.

"I'd like to talk about our future," Delia said gravely. Bridget paled, and Delia ran her thumb down her daughter's cheek. "I always wanted a big family. A big, happy family with children and a beautiful home in a beautiful neighborhood," Delia went on.

"You mean, you didn't dream of living in a haunted house?" Meryl grinned. "Aunt Viola has been inquiring about any vacancies, you know. Might want to be careful."

Delia laughed, as friends do when it came down to little ribbings here and there. In fact, they already *had* invited Viola into the house. She'd accepted and planned to move in the following spring, once the snow had begun to melt. With one extra bedroom, it would be no trouble to accept someone else who was looking for a place to call home.

"I always dreamed of living in a country club," Delia answered.

"What is a country club, anyway?" Bridget asked, reminding Delia of herself when she was young. Just before she and her mother got their big first break: cleaning a house in the Ocean City Seaside Club. It was everything to Delia, to have that experience, and to share it with her mom. And when her mom passed soon after, Delia was all the more crushed to lose that job. But once she arrived in Gull's Landing and learned that the whole world was far bigger than Ocean City—and especially the Seaside Club—she knew that she might fill a bigger space in it herself.

"What do you think it is?" Delia asked Bridget, twisting one of the girl's smooth black braids—her signature style, as Delia had deemed it when Bridget moved in and asked if she was going to have to dress differently. *Only if you want to*, Delia had answered. *I happen to like how you dress now, though.* It had meant something to the sweet child, and she kept braiding her hair each morning, out of familiarity and comfort and maybe in honor of the mother she once had. The one who taught her to braid. Who taught her all the things that helped her survive in the interim between then and now.

"I think it's a group of friends who live out in the country. And they have a club where they promise to always be friends and never leave each other. No matter what happens."

"If I didn't know any better, I'd say that sounds a lot like us, Bridget," Lucy remarked from behind her steaming mug.

"It is us," Bridget replied. Then her eyes flashed up at Delia. "Your dream came true."

Delia, drunken with good food and hot cocoa and joy, shook her head, clearing the fog of her bliss. "What, sweetheart?"

It was Meryl, though, who answered, leaning back into John's arms as they cuddled on the loveseat together. "You live in a country club again," she said, grinning.

Delia smiled contentedly. "I suppose that's true." She

glanced at her no-longer-new best friend. "Meryl, what about you? Do you have any dreams?"

"Only my fair share." Meryl smirked.

"I think I got everything I ever dreamed of," Lucy interjected.

"You're lucky," Bridget pointed out. "Most people don't even get half of what they dream of."

"That reminds me," Meryl said. "Did you know my parents opened a scholarship at Shearwater? They paid into it whenever they had spare money. It was probably part of their financial demise, but the penance was important to them."

Bridget shrugged. "I knew your last name. Maybe I heard about it." Now that she was ten, Bridget was testing the boundaries of her confidence and the extent of her *coolness*.

John shook his head. "You probably wouldn't know about this one. It's a private scholarship. And sort of a... a reverse one," he said, frowning seriously.

"What's a reverse scholarship?" Delia asked. "Shearwater is funded by the state, right? What girl needs a scholarship to get in? Aren't they... *placed*?"

"It covers the adoption fees and associated expenses for one girl per year," Meryl answered, repeating what John had explained to her before.

Delia stared hard at Meryl. "What are you saying?"

"I'm saying, the Preston Family Adoption Scholarship has chosen who it will sponsor this year." Meryl pushed up from the sofa and crossed to the Christmas tree, a full-bodied green fir, beneath which were littered a variety of pretty-papered presents. She selected a small, golden-wrapped box with a puffy red bow tied around it.

"This is for you, Bridget. And you, Delia," Meryl said as she kneeled in front of Bridget and passed her the gift. "From the Mill River Road Country Club Room Renters' Association, you could say." She bit her lower lip and winked at the girl.

Bridget seemed nervous. Her hands trembled as she worked free the ribbon. It unfurled into her lap. Delicately, she peeled away the paper to reveal a white box, the lid of which she removed slowly, peeking inside as if whatever was within might pop out at her like a Jack-in-the-Box.

Bridget lifted two medallions from the box and studied them curiously.

"Saint William, the patron saint of adopted children. For you, Bridget. And Saint Monica, the patron saint of mothers. For you, Delia," Meryl whispered and retreated to the loveseat, a small smile on her mouth.

Bridget looked up, first at Delia then at Meryl. Delia mirrored her, staring again at Meryl. "Does this mean—"

"I know your real dream wasn't the country club one. And anyway, that one came true," Meryl replied.

"You're like me, Delia," Lucy added, squeezing Marcia's hand on her knee as they sat side by side on the sofa. "All you wanted in the world was a little girl of your own."

"And if it's what you both want," John went on, "then it's what you can have."

Delia looked at Bridget. "Is this what you want?"

"A home forever and a mother? A family again?" Bridget's eyes were wet and her lips quaking. "It's all I've wanted in a long, long time."

"There now," Meryl said as Delia and Bridget squeezed each other tight. "Everyone's gotten what they want most in the world. Right?"

"Only our fair share," Lucy said mischievously, mimicking Meryl.

Meryl, herself, felt emotional. It would be her second Christmas as an orphan. And that would never change. No matter what. Even if Lucy was a bit like a mother to her. Even if she had her best friend, Delia, just downstairs. Even if Aunt Viola did move in and she had John and her new job and all the things in the world that her own parents would have wanted for her.

Lucy saw it in Meryl's eyes. The one thing she couldn't have. The one thing Meryl would never get, no matter what. A chance to change the past. A chance to say *yes* to her mother. Rather than no. One last chance.

"Meryl," Lucy said, her expression even and her voice soft. "Did I ever tell you I met your mother once?"

Meryl studied her. "You said you *didn't* know my mom," she replied.

"I didn't know her, no. But I met her. She came to Shearwater just after the accident."

Her heart pounding in her chest, Meryl willed herself to stay calm. "She did?"

Lucy nodded. "She must have been pregnant with you. She cupped her belly and waddled slightly. Though there wasn't an obvious bump, it was obvious she was protecting something in there. You, I now know."

"You never mentioned this," Meryl accused.

"I didn't know what your plans were. I didn't want this to affect them. I knew your mother wouldn't have wanted them to."

"What? What are you talking about?" Meryl asked Lucy. The room was silent save for the flickering of the fire and the incessant, calming purring from Fiona.

"She asked the headmaster if she could contribute in some way to Shearwater, perhaps by moving back into the house. She said she'd clean it or take one of the girls or do whatever she could to make up for the tragedy." Lucy swallowed a sip of her cocoa. "I was there, in the room. The headmaster told her that nothing she could do would bring back that girl. And she was best suited to selling the property and staying far away."

"They didn't want her to stay?" Meryl asked, confused by this.

"He was angry. We all were. But I remember the last thing she said before she left his office."

"What?" Charlie asked Lucy, as rapt as everyone else in the room.

Lucy leaned forward from the sofa, her gaze heavy on Meryl. "She said she'd never forgive herself for what happened. That she would regret it for the rest of her life. She would regret not having the house bulldozed or fixed —neither of which she could afford. Anyway, locally, this house is on the National Register of Historic Homes."

"You're kidding," Meryl answered.

Lucy shook her head. "People might have forgotten by now. The Stevers Country Home. There used to be a placard. It was probably stolen. Anyway, to tear it down was impossible. And to fix it would require special permits and more money than they had, I'm sure. And your mother regretted all of it. I mean, I think she did what she could. New floor. Locks. But she carried a lot of guilt, as you now know."

"But it wasn't her fault. She didn't know what would happen," Meryl protested

Lucy eased back onto the sofa, a satisfied look on her face. "That's my point, my child," she said. "Your mother is watching down on you now, Meryl. She wants you to know that *she* knows you loved her. And maybe she's sorry, too. Maybe both of you made some mistakes, but that doesn't change a mother's love for her child." Lucy took up Marcia's hand again. "And it surely doesn't change the fact that a mother always feels her child's love for her, too. No matter what."

At that, Meryl sobbed. Body-wracking sobs that consumed her and expelled all the hurt and the pain that she'd pent up over the course of eighteen months. The sorrow that had mounted inside of her. And when she was done, when she was good and cried out and John and all the others had comforted her, they opened gifts.

And that was when Meryl realized what it was she had always wanted.

A soft place to fall.

*A group of friends who lived out in the country. Who had a club where they promised to always be friends and never leave each other. No matter what happened.*

If you enjoyed this story, be sure to order the author's newest women's fiction, *The House on Apple Hill Lane.* Join Elizabeth Bromke's reader club today at elizabethbromke.com.
Looking for a different read? Check out the bestselling series, *Birch Harbor.*

## ALSO BY ELIZABETH BROMKE

Birch Harbor:

*House on the Harbor*

*Lighthouse on the Lake*

*Fireflies in the Field*

*Cottage by the Creek*

*Bells on the Bay*

Gull's Landing:

*The Summer Society, a USA Today Bestseller*

*The Garden Guild*

*The Country Club*

Harbor Hills:

*The House on Apple Hill Lane*

*The House with the Blue Front Door*

The Hickory Grove Series

## ACKNOWLEDGMENTS

Thank you Elise Griffin with Edits by Elise for polishing another fun story. Your notes were supremely helpful. And Tandy Oschadleus, thank you for your eagle eye. I couldn't do this without you both!

My family is ever supportive, and I am so grateful to them. Especially my mom, dad, brother, sisters, mothers-in-law and fathers-in-law. But also my extended family—including the Bromke and Fiorillo broods. Thank you!

I am fortunate to have readers who have endeared themselves to me as friends. Either by email or social media, we've connected, and I've pulled inspiration from your support. Without my readers, I'd be lost. Thank you for buying my stories and for accepting them and even loving them. Your glowing reviews and kind words kindle my fire. Not only that, but our correspondences helps me shape the female friendships I write about. I pour over your messages. Keep them coming!

My husband is not only my biggest supporter. He's

also my best friend, business partner, and everything else that a man can be. I love you so much, Ed!

Eddie... you know this: always for you.

# ABOUT THE AUTHOR

After graduating from the University of Arizona, Elizabeth Bromke became an English teacher. You can still find her in a classroom today, behind a stack of essays and a leaning tower of classic novels.

When she's not teaching, Elizabeth writes women's fiction and contemporary romance. For fun, she enjoys jigsaw puzzles, crosswords, and—of course—reading.

Elizabeth lives in the northern mountains of Arizona with her husband, son, and their sweet dog Winnie.

Learn more about the author by visiting her website at elizabethbromke.com.

Made in the USA
Las Vegas, NV
20 April 2021

21474348R00135